Anitbeet Productions Presents

Hoop

Dreams

Deflated

a novel by

Yani

Yani

Hoop Dreams Deflated

By Yani

Published by Anitbeet Productions

ISBN **978-0-9969666-7-2**

Printed in the U.S.A

Pre-Game

I remember the first basketball game I watched as a young buck. I was five years old and LeBron James was a rookie playing for the Cavaliers, who were cooking the Sixers. I sat on our living room floor in our old house on Medary Street watching the 27-inch Zenith television with the fat back. Pops had just gotten cable for us and while my little sister and I should have been watching cartoons, we were both tuned into the game, cheering as though we had courtside seats. Watching LeBron dominate on the floor amazed me, and I vowed as I watched that game that one day, I was going to make it to the NBA as well.

Yani

Roaches crawled down the dingy walls in the living room of the three-bedroom house we were currently living in. Janaya, who was two at the time, pointed at one as she squealed, "Ewww! Rooooach!" I scooted close to the bug and squashed it with an envelope like I had seen Mommy do numerous times. She frowned but then went back to playing with her doll baby. I sighed and cupped my chin in my hands while sitting Indian style on the dirty, carpeted floor.

Once again, we were home alone, left behind by our mother who more than likely was out at some bar. She promised she was going to bring us back some Chinese Food for dinner. Though I couldn't quite tell time yet, I knew she'd left just as the game had started and it was now the third quarter, so she had to have been gone for over an hour.

My stomach growled loudly and I closed my eyes trying not to think about how hungry I was. Janaya was just as hungry as I was, if not more.

"Dah-Dah… C'ave some?" she asked me as she pulled on my shirt. It was her way of saying "Davion, can I have some?" "Dah-Dah" is what she called me since she couldn't pronounce my name. I looked over at her angrily but her soft brown eyes and thick, curly bush made me calm down. I had already told her three times that we had to wait for mommy to come back with the food, but she was hungry now, and we couldn't wait anymore. We shouldn't have to wait anymore.

"Alright Janaya, let me see what's in the kitchen," I said to her with a smile. But I knew there was hardly anything in there. I got up just as the Sixers were calling time-out and went into the kitchen. Janaya followed behind me. The kitchen's only measly light blinked off and on as though the bulb was about to blow out. I cringed as I looked around at the grimy, dirty stove. The linoleum on the floor was supposed to be a soft pink and egg-shell color, but since Mr. Clean hadn't seen these floors in probably a year, the floor was dirty and grimy with old, crusted grease caked up near the stove and the cabinet under the sink. Roaches scattered around the sink that was filled with dirty dishes from more than a week ago. I opened the refrigerator and frowned at the smell that seeped out from the old food and spoiled milk that should have been thrown out weeks ago. My stomach growled again and I was beginning to feel sick.

Janaya squeezed past me so she could see inside of the refrigerator and then pointed to the jar of grape jelly.

"It's no bread, Jah-Jah," I said to her. I guess her determination was greater than mine and maybe she was a little braver than me because she yanked on one of the vegetable bin drawers, pulling it open. Inside was some bread. I grabbed it along with the jelly and pulled it out, excited. But when I opened the bag, I saw that the bread on top was molded.

"Ill…" I groaned. At that moment, my hate for my mother became stronger than any emotion I could remember having towards anyone at five years old. Janaya was still excited, thinking we would be able to have jelly sandwiches. I pulled the first slice off and threw it in the trash before checking again. I ended up having to throw most of the bread away, but the slices in the middle and towards the bottom were still salvageable.

There were no clean spoons in the drawers to the cabinet near the sink, so I dug into the pile of filthy dishes and grabbed the cleanest, dirty spoon

I could find. I rinsed it off, scraping the crusted food bits from it before drying it on my shirt and made my baby sister and I sandwiches.

Just as we were chowing down and filling our hungry bellies with the yummy snack, the lights fluttered again only this time, they cut all the way off.

"NYEARRRONNN!" was the noise the power made before the house went completely dark. Janaya screamed and I shushed her. I could feel her tiny arms cling to me out of fear of the dark. I strained to see in the pitch-black kitchen, using my hands to find the rest of our sandwiches on the kitchen counter before we made our way to the living room, with Janaya clinging to me the whole way there. The lights in there were off as well, and the TV too. Now I was scared, also.

"Dah-Dah, I want Mommy!" Janaya cried. The silence of the house accentuated her tearful cries making them seem louder than usual.

"Be quiet before the neighbors hear us! Shhh, Janaya!" I said, trying to calm her down.

I pulled the curtains back a little bit and saw when the Peco Energy worker placed an envelope in our mailbox before leaving our porch. Using the light from the street lights in the front of our house, I was able to find the house phone. I said Pop's number in my head the way he taught it to me as I dialed it. I waited while it rang, peering from behind the curtains, trying to keep watch for Mommy, knowing that if she caught me calling him, she would beat me senseless. But we were hungry, home alone, cold, and the Peco man just turned our lights out.

"What?" Pops said into the phone with base as though he was expecting it to be our mother.

"Da… Daddy?" I said with a stutter, a bad habit that I had at the time whenever I was scared.

"Oh, hey son. Sorry about that. Wassup?" my father said, softening his voice.

"Nuh…noth… nothing. Me… me and Juh… Janaya are in the house buh… buh…by ourselves and thuh… thuh… thuh… the Peco muh… muh… man just tuh… tuh… turned off the lights." I took a deep breath trying not to cry on the phone. I didn't want my dad to think I was a punk.

I heard Pops sigh angrily over the phone. "Where the hell is your mom?" he asked.

"I don't know. She said sh… sh… she was guh… guh… getting us suh… suh… some Chinese Food buh… buh… but she didn't get back yet."

I could hear some shuffling around where I guess my dad was trying to muffle the phone so I couldn't hear what he was saying.

"Babe, swing me around Medary street so I can get my kids. This bitch done left my fucking kids in the house with nothing to eat and they done turned the muthafucking lights off. I'm so sick of this fucking broad man, she really 'bout to make me fuck her up over my kids, man!" he hissed. I heard a woman respond back but couldn't make out what she said.

"Get your little sister, I'll be there in like five minutes."

"Oh… Oh-kay." I said before hanging the phone up. Just hearing that my pops was going to come rescue us from this messed up situation gave me a burst of energy. I grabbed onto Janaya and kissed her cheek. "Daddy's coming to get us," I said with a huge grin on my face.

"Yaaayyyy!" Janaya shouted with glee. We both climbed onto the sofa and watched out the window for his arrival. It seemed like forever, but then this really dope, hunter-green Nissan Maxima pulled up blasting 50 Cent's cut *In Da Club*. As soon as I saw my father hop out of the passenger seat, I grabbed Janaya in my arms and hurried to the front door.

"Daddy!" Janaya said with glee as he scooped her into his arms.

"Hey baby-girl! Gimme 'dem kisses, boop." He made fart noises on her cheeks causing her to laugh loudly before grabbing me by the head and pulling me close. He felt me shiver.

"Where y'all coats?" He then looked down at me and looked at Janaya. "Ay yo, why ya'll dressed all dirty like this and where the fuck are y'all shoes?"

I opened my mouth to tell Pops that I couldn't find our coats and shoes in the house because it was too dark, and we were dressed in what mommy had us wearing for the last three days when I saw our mother coming up the street. My eyes widened in fear.

"What the fuck are you doing at my house?" she sneered as she marched over to the porch. "Davion, what I tell you about opening my fucking door for folks without me telling you to?" she sniped at me. I scooted behind my father, using his leg to hide from her.

"Y'all go get in the car," my father said to us as he put Janaya down. "I'ma take y'all shopping, okay? How's that sound, y'all like that?" he asked us with a smile as he knelt in front of us. We nodded our heads rapidly.

"You not takin' my muthafuckin' kids no got-damn where! Fuck is you thinking?" My mother snapped with her head wagging back and forth. I could tell she was trying hard not to stagger as I looked back at her while Pops' girlfriend helped us get into the car. I also noticed that she didn't have any Chinese Food with her either.

The inside of the car was crisp clean with cream leather seats. The TVs in the headrest were turned on for me and Janaya while we snuggled close to each other, waiting for the heat in the car to work its magic on our chilly bodies. Shrek came on and Janaya tuned in, oblivious to the argument our mother and father were having outside.

"I know got-damn well you ain't bring yo' bitch to my house, nigga. What fuckin' tip are you on?" my mother hissed.

Yani

"Bitch, you left my fucking kids in the house with nothing to eat by they-self while you out drinking and getting high and the fucking lights just got turned off! What the fuck did you do with the money I gave you, huh? Why my fucking son looking like he ain't had a hair-cut in months, and Janaya looking like her shit ain't been combed in who-the-fuck-knows how long?" My father tore into our mother. I could see the neighbors cracking their doors open and peeking outside to see what was going on.

My mother waved her hand in the air in a dismissive manner. "Nigga, don't question me about what the fuck I do. I take care of these kids. That little bitta-ass money you gave me don't stretch but so far."

"Man, fuck outta here," My father said as he turned to walk off the porch. He zipped his grey hooded Akademic sweatshirt up and pulled the hoodie up over his head.

"Wait, nigga where the fuck is you takin' my kids?" My mother hurried after him.

"Yo, Joselyn I ain't for your shit man, you better go the fuck 'head. They coming with me, fuck is you talking about?" my father replied as he looked at her as though she was crazy.

"Not-ine, nigga, take my fucking kids outta that bitch's car, right now!"

My father's girlfriend whipped her head in my mother's direction and before I knew it, she was out the car.

"Who the fuck you think you talkin' to? Bitch? Bitch? Yo, I will mop the fucking block up with your crackhead ass, boo-boo! You got me fucking chopped!"

Pops jumped in between them just as they were about to come to blows. He hemmed Meagan up against the car. "Watch ya mouth yo! That's my kids' mom, I got this."

"You betta check that girl. She got the right one tonight." Meagan said angrily.

"I got this yo, just get back in the car, man, chill!"

"Don't think 'cause you fuckin' that nigga that mean shit, bitch. You ain't the only one! You ain't the only one! Believe 'dat, bitch! Believe 'dat!" My mom shouted. My father turned towards my mother and gripped her up by her collar. She swung her tiny arms at him, trying to push him off her as she yelled for him to let her go, but he shoved her back to her porch.

"You a sorry excuse for a mother and a waste of fucking oxygen. It's a good thing I love my babies, 'cause had I known you woulda turned out like this, I woulda just nutted in your mouth. If you want these fucking kids, you better take me to court. But as long as you out here on that shit, snorting that shit, smoking it, whatever-the-fuck-you doing, you ain't never getting these kids back. Now, believe 'dat shit! Believe 'dat!" he said, mocking her.

And with those words, my pops came back to the car. He opened the driver side door and motioned for Meagan to get out. He apologized for the disrespect she endured at the hands of our mother before giving her a kiss. He then took the wheel and she got in on the passenger side. I watched as the two of them held hands.

Meagan had always been nice to us the few times that we had been around her, and I secretly wished she was our mother instead of Joselyn. But as the saying goes, you can pick your nose, but you can't pick your family.

Hoop Dreams Deflated

I fell asleep in the back of the car, dreaming about playing for the hottest team in the NBA and being one of the most talked about players. My dream was interrupted when my father tapped me on my shoulder. I squinted and stretched before my eyes were finally able to focus on him.

"Come on boy so you can eat dinner. But first, I want you and your sister to come outta those dirty-ass clothes so y'all can get in the tub, a'ight?" he said to me with a serious look on his face.

"Alright, Dad." I replied as I opened the door to get out. He scooped Janaya up in his arms and carried her to the house. She had also fallen asleep in the back of the car and rested her head on his shoulder, clinging to him as the cold night air chilled her body.

We walked up a neatly paved walkway attached to a freshly cut front lawn that was lined with green hedges. I looked around and was in awe at how clean the block was. Everyone's grass was freshly cut and their hedges were neatly trimmed. There was no trash on the ground, and the porch lights made the block look cheerful even on this cold, dark night.

Yani

"This where you live, Dad?" I asked as I looked up at my father while we walked up the pathway.

"Yeah, Meagan and I just got this house about a month ago. I wanted to get everything straight in here before I brought y'all here, nah-mean? Make sure y'all rooms were tight. We're not done, but it's still cool."

"Man… I wish we lived here," I sulked.

My father was quiet for a moment as Meagan unlocked the door. He held it open so we could all go inside. "Well, if things work out, y'all can stay with me permanently. You know what that word means, son?"

"Don't it mean like, forever?" I guessed with an unsure look on my face.

He smiled at me and nodded his head. "You a smart lil' dude. Yeah, it's kinda like that, but the exact definition is when something remains unchanged for all time." He laid Janaya down on the couch and then stood back up to face me. "See, your pops was smart back in school, too. I shoulda went to college but well…" he trailed off and shrugged his shoulders. "I'ma make sure you have that opportunity when you get older so you can be smarter than me, make better choices than I made, and just be an all-around better man than I am."

"I don't think anybody could ever be smarter than you, Pops." I said to my father with a smile.

He took me upstairs and showed me to my room which was mad dope. There was a basketball hoop on the back door, posters of Kobe Bryant, Allen Iverson, LeBron James and Dwyane Wade on the wall. My bed had big pillows on it with Pokémon sheets and a comforter, and there was also a nightstand next to my bed with a cool lamp with swirly stuff inside that changed colors.

"Cool, dad!" I exclaimed as I pointed to it. "What's that?"

"It's called a lava lamp. But look," he said as he turned out the light. Dinosaurs appeared in the same colors as the ones in the lava lamp on the ceiling and they looked as though they were moving around.

"Wowwwww!" I said as I stared up at the ceiling completely mesmerized. Back at my mother's house, the only thing that ever moved around on my ceiling were roaches, and I didn't even have a bed. I had a mattress that I slept on with Janaya.

My father turned the light back on, snapping me out of my thoughts before giving me a pat on my head. "Meagan is running you a bath. Come out of those clothes so I can throw them out. There's some underwear, undershirts and pajamas in the top dresser drawer."

I nodded my head and began to slowly undress, hoping my father would leave the room.

"Why you moving so slow, boy? Hurry up so Janaya can get in the tub too, and y'all can eat dinner."

I looked up at my father nervously but moved faster. I tried to peel my pants and underwear down together and ball them up so he couldn't see the condition they were in. He frowned up his nose.

"Ay yo… you don't wipe yourself when you go to the bathroom?" he asked me with a frown on his face.

I opened my mouth to speak but closed it as I lowered my head in shame. My underwear was soiled with thick poop stains and the smell permeated throughout the room.

Hoop Dreams Deflated

Pops shook his head in disgust before reaching in the hall closet and grabbing a trash bag. "Put those in there. Listen, I know things were crazy at your mom's house. But all that is going to change while you're here, understand? I'ma teach you what I wasn't able to teach you since I wasn't in the house with y'all, and the first thing is, you gotta wipe ya' ass when you take a shit, understand?" my father said to me as he passed me a towel, a washcloth and a bar of soap. I nodded my head trying to overcome the shame of having my father see my underwear as they were and smell me like he had just done.

He helped me get in the tub and instead of letting me wash myself, he washed me himself as he talked to me, schooling me about the importance of having good personal hygiene as well as explaining how I needed to properly wash while always keeping a fresh haircut, and making sure my clothes and sneakers were always neat and clean. He stressed the importance of always looking my best not just for the "ladies" as he put it, but because it would make me feel good about myself. I took in everything my father said to me while I

Yani

was in the tub, promising myself that I would be the best I could be just for him. I admired and respected my father so much from that moment on, wanting to be just like him. I knew I would look like him when I got older. He was extremely tall, probably as tall as LeBron, and was thick. We both had the same light-brown complexion only he had dimples and I didn't. The twinkle in his dark eyes probably dazzled the ladies, but to me and Janaya, that twinkle let us know that we were safe and everything would be alright from that point on.

That night, we sat at the dinner table like a family; me, Janaya, Pops, and Meagan. We ate pizza in the brightly lit dining room while ESPN played the highlights to that night's Sixers' loss against the Cavs, laughing at the jokes our father told.

As I was laying in my new bed staring up at the cool dinosaurs that moved about over my head, Janaya came into my room dragging the teddy bear that Meagan gave her. I wasn't surprised since she had been sleeping in the bed with me for more than a year. She climbed up on my bed and laid her head on my chest just as she had done at the other house before sticking her thumb in her mouth and falling asleep. Yeah, things were definitely going to be all right from now on.

Yani

1ˢᵗ Quarter

"Hurry up, Janaya!" I yelled to my baby sister as

I stood outside our father's house bouncing my

basketball. It was four years later and we were

living with Pops and Meagan fulltime, but visited

Joselyn on the weekends. They fought in court

over us for over a year before the judge finally let

me testify on me and Janaya's behalf. After telling

the judge about us being left in the house by

ourselves with no food, the way the house was

always left in a dirty, nasty condition and spoke of

the time the electric got cut off while she was out

drinking and getting high, the judge ruled in Pops

favor and granted sole custody to him.

I still remember how my mother broke down

in tears like one of us had died. At that moment, I

felt sorry for her. She promised us that she would

do better and she would "get her shit together" so

that we could be back home with her where we

belonged. I believe her at first, but later on, I knew she was only making those empty promises because no kids meant no welfare check.

Nevertheless, Pops didn't want to cut Joselyn out of our lives like that, which I believe he should have. Things would have been better if he had just severed ties with that crackhead bitch and raised us with Meagan. But even though he would never admit it, I believed Joselyn was still a soft spot for him and he had hopes that she could be the good woman he always imagined she'd be. He would never leave Meagan for her though, that much I knew. But I guess some stupid sappy side to him still had love for her. I, on the other hand, hated that bitch with a passion.

So, Pops talked things over with Joselyn and told her that she could have us every other weekend. His whole thing was, kids need their mother and their father. Meagan was a better substitution, but whatever. Janaya was all too pleased to see the woman she still calls "mommy". But whenever we go over there, I spend as much time away from that house as I can.

Yani

I dribbled the ball between my legs before stopping and letting out an annoyed sigh. "Come on, man!" I yelled again

"I'm coming, Dah-Dah, dang!" Janaya hissed. Even though she could fully say my name now, "Dah-Dah" is what she insisted on calling me. She was the only one I would let get away with that. A couple of homies would call me that, too. But it was annoying when the little girls around Pops' and Joselyn's neighborhood called me that.

A lot of people say Janaya and I look like twins even though we are three years apart. She's pretty tall for her age, standing close to my height. We both looked just like Pops spit us out and Joselyn had nothing to do with birthing us, which was cool to me. The less association I had with that woman, the better.

Janaya's hair was super thick and long. Meagan had taken her to the salon earlier to get it pressed and braided and they took like five freaking hours before they finally got back. I wanted to hurry up and get around the old way to hang with my homies before Joselyn tried to kick that curfew shit.

Hoop Dreams Deflated

Janaya ran out of the house with her Bratz book bag on her back with her long-beaded braids swinging back and forth. Her face glowed with Coco-butter and if I didn't know any better, she had a glossy look to her lips. She ran up on me as though she was playing defense and I dribbled the ball back and forth between my legs as she posted up.

"Unh, take that…. Up… too slow!" I laughed as I did a mini cross over. Janaya laughed but stayed with me and before I knew it, she smacked the ball from my hand and dribbled it away from me.

"Oh! That's my Lil' Mama! Go 'head Boop!" Pops said as he came out of the house. He locked the door behind him and walked over to us giving Janaya a pound. "You better watch it, Davion. She gon' mess around and be better than you if you don't tighten up," he said with a chuckle.

"It's cool, Pops. That's when you know I've done a good job teaching her when the student out does the master." I smiled back. My father tapped his fist against mine in midair.

"My man," he said in approval. He looked us over to make sure we were neat and clean before

Yani

nodding his head in approval. He always kept us fresh to death with the latest, flyest lays. We kept our best clothes at his house though, and rocked the plain stuff to Joselyn's house. I had on a pair of high-top black and grey Air Max's with a pair of gap jeans and a black and white striped long-sleeved polo shirt. Janaya was wearing a pair of pink and blue New Balances with a pair of Gap Jeans and a pink graphic long sleeved shirt with her jean jacket. We climbed in the back of Pops' Chevy Tahoe and he pulled off blasting T.I's *"Top Back Remix"*.

We maneuvered through the streets on that sun shiny day going from the Cedarbrook section of the city to nut-ass G-Town. It was Spring Break and the kids were out and about playing tag-football, jumping rope, and riding their bikes. I hated the neighborhood that Joselyn lived in, but some of my team mates were from around the way so I hung with them. To make sure the fast-ass little girls in the neighborhood didn't try anything, I kept Janaya with me.

We pulled up on the block and Pops parked. I had an instant attitude and he could see it in my face.

"What's the problem, Davion?" he asked me as he turned around to look at us.

"Why we gotta come here?" I asked with a frown.

"We go through this every time and I'm getting tire of this," Pops said to me sternly.

"I'm getting tired of coming here," I mumbled in a smart tone.

"Ay, who the hell you think you talking to, boy? You better check yourself, I ain't one of your friends." Pops said with base in his voice. I immediately humbled myself. "Now you know the routine and I done explained the situation to you, which was a courtesy because you a little-ass boy and I really don't have to explain shit to you. You just do what the hell I say, got that?!" he said loudly.

"Yes sir," I mumbled while looking at the floor of his truck.

"Regardless how you feel about her, she's still your mother and you better respect her as such. One day she won't be here and you're gonna wish like shit she was."

"*I doubt it,*" I thought to myself, knowing better than to say it out loud.

Yani

He reached in his pocket and handed each of us twenty dollars. Janaya had a huge grin on her face as she stuffed the money in her book bag. I folded mine up and put it in my back pocket.

"Come on. I gotta make some runs. Remember what I told y'all."

"Be respectful, be peaceful, set a good example for each other and look out for one another. Because attitude is a little thing that makes a big difference." Janaya and I said together. Pops nodded his head in approval and got out of the truck just as Joselyn was opening the front door. I secretly was hoping that she wasn't home so Pops would take us back home with him.

"Gimme kiss," he said to Janaya. She jumped in his arms as though she was still two-years-old and he picked her up before spinning her around, making her laugh out loud. He then made fart noises on her cheek and she did the same to him in return before he put her down. She ran over to Joselyn and gave her a hug.

"Don't give ya momma a hard time, boy. She's trying. And in this world, you can't fault a person who's trying to do better, and you can't make 'em feel like shit about their past either because that does more harm than good, understand?" he said as he knelt in front of me.

I sighed and nodded my head before tapping my fist against his. I then turned and headed towards "my mother."

"Hey Ma," I said plainly before giving her a hug. She squeezed me tightly.

"Hey baby. I heard your team won the other day. Sorry I didn't get to come to your game, I had a doctor's appointment to go to," she fumbled.

I shrugged my shoulders knowing she was lying. "It's cool," I replied in the same plain tone.

"You good?" Pops asked our mom.

"Yeah. How's things with you?" she asked in a surprisingly pleasant tone.

"Everything's straight on this end. Let me know if they need anything." Pops always kept it brief with her. She watched him as he got back in his truck and pulled off.

"I'm about to go hang with Lamar and 'nem." I said after dropping my book bag on the living room floor.

"Well damn, boy. You just got here and you already wanna run the streets. You can't sit down for a minute?" Joselyn frowned with a hand on her hip.

I huffed as I crossed my arms over my chest and leaned onto the raggedy couch she still had. I looked around and noticed that she had cleaned up a lot in there. I felt her staring at me and it began to annoy me so I huffed again.

She shook her head and waved her hand at me. "Fine, take your sister with you. But take those book-bags upstairs first and make sure you have your key."

I snatched me and Janaya's book bags up from off the floor and took them upstairs quickly. I then hurried downstairs and grabbed my basketball before we both ran from the house. I didn't know about Janaya, but I felt like a runaway slave who was getting my first taste of freedom.

"Don't stay out too late!" Joselyn yelled after us. I ignored her as Janaya and I ran around the corner to go to Lamar's house.

Lamar's mom was way different than Joselyn. Unlike our mother, Ms. Aretha actually gave a shit about where her son went, who he hung out with, and the rule at their house was "your ass better be on these steps when the street lights come on or

I'm coming for you." She fried the best chicken wings and made the best macaroni and cheese. I remember the first time she offered me and Janaya something to eat right before we went to go live with our father. I was mad embarrassed when I came into Lamar's house and saw how clean it was and the way it was decorated. It smelled sweet like she was baking a fresh apple pie. Their house, to me, is what every family's house should be like.

I completely felt out of place there because my clothes were bummy and I was dirty looking. But she was extremely nice to me and Janaya. And when we sat down at the table with her, held hands and said grace, I got a taste of what family life was supposed to be like. I tore that fucking food up, too. Ever since then, Lamar's house was always the house we went to whenever we had to come stay with Joselyn. When Pops found out how nice Ms. Aretha was to us, welcoming us in her home to play with Lamar on days when it was super cold outside and giving us dinner and snacks, that's when he started giving us a little more money and let me know as a young man, to never go to Ms. Aretha's house empty handed even if all I brought her was a Pepsi.

"Hey Davion and Janaya!" she said with a smile when she opened the door for us.

I dug the Pepsi out and gave it to her. "Here you go, Ms. Aretha. Is Lamar home?"

Ms. Aretha chuckled. "Boy, I keep telling you, you do not have to bring me a Pepsi or anything when you come over here. You keep that money for you and your sister," she said to me. "And yes, he's home. He's upstairs cleaning his room. I told him his ass isn't going anywhere until that damn room is cleaned."

"Janaya has her own money and I don't mind, Ms. Aretha. That's respect," I said with a charming smile. "I can help him clean his room." I volunteered.

"Sure, if you wanna go up in that pig sty, you go right ahead." We all laughed before I ran up the stairs to Lamar's room. Janaya went into the kitchen to help with dinner.

"What's up, Lamar?" I said to my friend as I came into his room. I looked around and whistled. "Damn, it look like a tornado hit this jawn."

Hoop Dreams Deflated

Lamar chuckled before stepping over a messy pile of clothes to give me a handshake. Even though I volunteered to help him clean his room, I had no idea where I was going to begin.

"I don't think we're going to finish in time to go play ball today. It's already after 5 o'clock." I said to him.

"Yeah, we probably won't. But we can just play the PS3 instead." Lamar suggested. That was cool with me.

We separated dirty clothes from the clean clothes, putting the dirty ones in his hamper and folding the clean ones up and putting them in his dresser drawers while we talked about basketball. Almost two hours later, the room was finished with the exception of us having to vacuum. I could smell the fried fish that Ms. Aretha was making downstairs and it made my stomach growl. We heard a tapping on Lamar's door.

"Yo!" he called out.

Janaya opened the door and peeked in. "Ms. Aretha said dinner will be ready in five minutes so wash y'all hands so you can come eat."

Yani

"Alright, here we come," Lamar replied as he moved his bed so we could vacuum under it.

"Oh, and she said don't even think about hiding anything in the closet or under the bed 'cause she will be checking," Janaya said, imitating Lamar's mom. She almost sounded just like her.

"Alright man, chill!" We all laughed as Janaya closed the door. Lamar and I looked at each other and quickly pulled trash from under the dresser and in the closet before dumping it in a bag.

"Damn yo, how did she know?" I asked.

Lamar huffed, "She's a mom. Moms always knows."

"Shit, my mom wouldn't have known. Doubt she would've cared either.

Lamar was quiet for a moment before responding. "Chris said he saw your mom copping from Slice the other day."

That wasn't news to me. I had known for the last three years that my mom was on something more than just E&J and weed. But I didn't care. That was her life.

"Yeah," was the only thing I said with a sigh. Lamar peeked over at me before turning the vacuum on and hitting the areas under his bed and behind his door. We then washed our hands and went downstairs to eat dinner.

The tilapia fish was a golden brown with just the right crispiness around the edges and seasoned perfectly. She made dirty rice and string beans that had a buttery taste to them. The sweet and warm Hawaiian roles completed the meal and we washed it down with tall glasses of lemonade. Janaya and I helped clear the table. I offered to wash the dishes while Lamar went to set up the PS3, but Ms. Aretha declined my offer. I noticed Janaya was checking her pockets and her jacket as though she was looking for something.

"What's the problem, Jah-Jah?" I asked her.

"I can't find my money..." she grumbled as she searched her jacket.

"You put it in your book bag, remember?" I reminded her. She looked at me with her mouth gaped open and then pouted.

"Aww man. I wanted an ice-cream Snickers from the store," she whined.

"Don't worry about it, I got you," I said to her. I then asked Ms. Aretha if it was okay for Lamar to walk us to the store. She gave him the okay and off we went. I blew through the money left from the Pepsi I bought Ms. Aretha earlier buying snacks for all three of us. We were on our way back to the house when we noticed a group of boys standing on the corner. Lamar sucked his teeth.

"I hope they don't start no shit today. I ain't in the mood, man." Lamar said in a low voice. I looked all of the guys over not really recognizing them from the neighborhood and continued eating my chips, not really paying them any mind.

"Ay yo, ya name Dah-Dah?" one of the guys asked me just as we were passing them.

I turned around annoyed. Only a few select people were allowed to call me that. "Yeah, why wassup?"

"Ain't ya mom Joselyn?" the same boy asked me with a smirk on his face.

"Yeah, why wassup?" I asked again wondering what the point was.

"Oh, my mans told me she was at the trap house giving neck for dime bags," the guy tried to maintain a straight face as his friends burst out laughing. Lamar pulled on my arm, encouraging me to let it go and keep walking. I was hot inside and wanted to knock the young bol's teeth out of his mouth. Even though I didn't bang with my mom like that, I wasn't about to start letting niggas on the street disrespect her. I shook my head and turned with Lamar to continue back to his house.

"Come on, Jah-Jah," I said to my little sister. She was looking at the boys in disgust.

"Shit, I might as well let that bitch suck my dick, too," another boy said causing them all to roar with laughter. "Them crack whores put in work."

"Don't be talking about my mom like that!" Janaya said in a loud squeaky voice. Even though she was only six, she was explosive like a fire cracker when set off.

"Shut up you lil bitch. You can eat a dick, too," the same boy snarled at my little sister. He really fucked up now.

Lamar grabbed my arm when he saw me drop my bags and move towards the main guy with the loud mouth. "Come on, Davion, it ain't even worth it."

"Nah fuck that," I said as I continued to the guy. "You better watch how you talk to my little sister." I said when I got close to him.

Yani

"Fuck you gon' do. You betta take ya dirty ass back to Medary street," the boy challenged.

Before I knew it, I had cocked my fist back and popped him dead in his mouth. We started fighting. It was my first street fight but I was landing some good punches. I guess his friends didn't appreciate him getting beat up because a couple of them jumped in it.

"Get off my brother!" I heard Janaya scream, and before I knew it, she had jumped in it as well. One of the boys smacked her and pushed her to the ground but she got right back up and fought back.

A few adults who were nearby ran over to us and broke everything up. By that time, someone had stolen the snacks that I bought from the store for me and Janaya. I wasn't pissed about that, though. I was pissed that Lamar was supposed to be my friend and really stood there and let them jump me. My baby sister had more heart than him.

"Yo, that was fucked up!" I yelled at Lamar, huffing and puffing, trying to catch my breath as I checked Janaya to make sure she was okay. She had a couple scratches but nothing major. I could look at her and tell she wanted to cry but she held her own.

"How?" Lamar yelled back. "I told you to just keep it moving, but you wanna be swinging on them niggas."

"So, you just gon' sit there and let them jump me? Seriously!" I asked back in disbelief.

"What was I supposed to do?" Lamar asked stupidly.

I looked at Lamar as though he were the dumbest fucking kid on the block. "Dickhead, jump in it and help me, that's what. Like yo, if that was you getting rolled on, I would've jumped in that shit for you!" I didn't usually curse that much but I was pissed.

"Man, whatever. I ain't getting rolled on because you wanna be mad over something somebody said about your mom. You know what she be out here doing."

I looked at Lamar for a couple of seconds and was tempted to beat his ass right there. But it was at that moment that I knew he was not a real friend and would never be somebody I could depend on when shit got real. I sealed my lips while we continued back to his house.

Yani

"Oh my goodness, what happened?" Ms. Aretha asked when she saw us after we came back into the house.

"Nothing," I mumbled. "Jah-Jah, get your jacket so we can go home." I grabbed my basketball from out of the corner while I waited for my baby sister to get her jacket.

Ms. Aretha looked at her son and then looked at me and Janaya. "Something happened out there while going to the store. And where's your snacks?" she asked.

I still refused to say anything, too pissed to even begin telling her how much of a fucking coward her son was. Janaya threw her jacket on.

"Some boys called my momma a crackhead and Lamar let them jump my brother!" Janaya said angrily.

Ms. Aretha looked at Lamar shocked and then looked at us. Lamar opened his mouth to defend himself as he did with me, seeing his lack of action as justified, but his mother put her hand up to silence him.

"That's your friend, Lamar. He came here to visit you, helped you clean your room, more than likely bought you snacks from the store and you didn't help him while those boys were jumping him?!" she said, sounding like she was appalled.

Lamar's facial expression was priceless. I bet he couldn't believe his mother was siding with me. "I told him to just keep walking. He swung on the bol' first."

"That's besides the point! It would have been different if it had been a fair one on one fight and Davion lost. But you stood on the side line and watched your friend get jumped and wouldn't do anything? I raised you better than that!" Ms. Aretha scolded him. Good for his ass.

Lamar slumped down on the steps with his face twisted up in anger.

Ms. Aretha turned to me and Janaya. "Do you want me to walk you two home?" she asked us nicely.

"No, it's okay. Thanks anyway, though." I grabbed Janaya's hand and we left the house. It had already gotten dark outside and judging by the limited lighting in the house, I could tell Joselyn wasn't home.

Yani

"Is what that boy said about mommy true?" Janaya asked me as I put the key in the door and unlocked it.

I was quiet for a moment not knowing how to answer her. The mean part of me wanted to say "Hell yeah it's true. Mommy's a fucking dope fiend and I wouldn't be surprised if she really was sucking dick for her next fix." But I didn't want to taint the image that Janaya had in her head of our mother.

"No, he was just trying to start trouble," I lied. "Come on, let's watch a movie." We went upstairs to my room and I turned on Lilo and Stitch, which was Jah-Jah's favorite cartoon at the moment. Dad bought us our own beds to have at the house and Janaya had her own room, but she still insisted on sleeping in the room with me whenever we stayed in this house. It was something about her room that scared her.

While sitting on the bed, she grabbed her book bag and reached inside.

"Hey…" she said as though she was stumped. She checked the zipped-up pockets and inside the side pockets of her book bag. "Where's my money?!" she exclaimed. She turned her book bag upside down after taking her toys out and her change of clothes, but nothing came out. Big surprise there. That's why I never leave my money in my book bag. I always keep it in my pockets and when I take my jeans off for the night, I sleep with whatever money I have left underneath my pillow.

"Maybe you dropped it in the back of Dad's truck, or maybe it fell out in the back of the truck when you were getting out," I suggested, even though I knew better.

Janaya looked as though she was in deep thought, trying to remember whether or not she dropped it. I reached in my pocket and pulled out the rest of the money I had from the last time we went to the store and saw that I only had four dollars and some change left.

"Come on, we can run across the street real quick before the store closes and get your ice-cream Snickers," I told her as I made my way to the bedroom door. Her frown quickly turned upside down and she skipped across the room to catch up with me.

Just as we were making our way down the stairs, the front door opened and Joselyn came into the house. I stopped in the middle of the stairs with

Yani

Janaya behind me. I looked her over and could immediately tell that she was high.

She looked up at us with her eyes low. "Oh hey, baby. I was just about to check to see if you were still at Lamar's house," she said as she closed and locked the door behind her. She stood facing the door for a moment as though she was trying to get her bearings together.

"Did y'all eat? It's some left over spaghetti in the fridge if ya hungry." She sashayed over to the sofa in a wobbly manner before flopping down on it and laying her head back against the flattened pillows. I stared down at her in contempt before shaking my head. My mother was a dope whore and I was fighting harder for her than she was fighting for herself. That's not something a nine-year-old boy should have to worry about.

"Jah-Jah, go back upstairs and watch Lilo and Stitch while I help mommy. I'll get your ice-cream Snickers in a minute."

"But I wanted to go with you," Janaya whined.

"Go upstairs!" I yelled at her not meaning to. She whined some more and then stomped back up the steps.

"Ay! Stop yelling and making all that damn noise. Shit, I got a headache," Joselyn complained.

I came the rest of the way back down the stairs and walked over to her on the couch. I wanted to slap her high ass. I wanted to slap her and shake her and tell her to clean herself up and do what a mother is supposed to do. like come to her son's basketball games, or her daughter's awards' assemblies. Bake cookies for home and school, come to back to school night, help us with our homework. But I knew she wouldn't listen and I doubted that it would make any difference.

Looking at her in her zooted up stupor, I began to feel sorry for her and wondered what happened that caused her to start getting high. I reached for her shoes and began to untie them so I could take them off. She stirred and then looked at me with heavy eyes before smiling.

"I knew you didn't hate me," she mumbled. "Thank you, baby-boy."

"You're welcome, momma." I replied as I untied her other shoe and began pulling it off. I couldn't stop thinking about what the boys on the corner said about her, and the entire scene of him talking about my mom sucking dick in exchange for drugs began to eat away at me. I took a deep breath in hopes that it would keep the tears from falling. My eyes stung and I blinked them away as I lifted her legs up so she could lay across the couch and get some rest. She snored lightly while I reached in the closet and pulled out a throw blanket. I laid it over top of her and she snuggled up under it as I kissed her lightly on the forehead.

"I love you, ma…" I whispered before leaving the house and getting the ice-cream Snickers I promised Janaya.

The next morning, I heard someone knocking loudly on the front door. I jumped up out of my sleep with my heart racing in my chest. I was positive that it was the cops coming to get my mom and drag her away because of something she did to get her drugs.

"Joselyn, open the damn door!" I heard my father say. He was here early. Me and Janaya wasn't expecting him until Friday night. It was only Wednesday morning.

I grabbed a shirt from out of my book bag and threw on my slippers before hurrying down the stairs. Janaya was a heavy sleeper so she didn't hear anything that was going on. Sometime during the night, Joselyn must have gotten up from the couch and gone upstairs to her room to go to bed. I unlocked and opened the door for my father. He looked pissed.

"Where's your mom?" he asked as he walked inside of the house.

"I think she's in her room sleeping," I replied wondering what the hell was going on.

"Get your stuff, get your sister and let's go. I'm taking y'all the fuck home. Aretha called me and told me how you and your sister got jumped because these lil' young dickheads wanna be starting shit with you behind the shit your mom is doing, and I'm not fucking having it. Get your shit, let's go!" Pops said angrily with base in his voice. I scurried upstairs and woke Janaya up.

"Come on, daddy is here. We're going home," I told her as I shook her awake. She whined as she always does whenever she has to wake up before she wants to.

I heard my father as he came up the stairs. He pushed her door open causing it to bang up against the wall. Joselyn stirred in her sleep. My heart raced a mile a minute as I listened while trying to get me and Janaya dressed.

"Wake yo ass up!" Pops said in a loud voice. I heard Joselyn groan in her sleep. "I said get up!"

I peeked out of my room to see what was going on. Pops snatched the sheets back from Joselyn and started going through the things on her dresser. She realized what he was doing and jumped up to stop him.

"Nigga, don't be going through my stuff, what the hell is wrong with you?!" she hissed at him as she tried to stop him. Pops mugged her away and then pushed her onto the bed. He opened her dresser drawers and rummaged through them until he found what he was looking for. He held up a glass pipe.

"You still doing this shit around my fucking kids, huh? You still sucking on this glass dick and getting high around my fucking kids!" Pops yelled in a voice I had never heard before. It terrified me. He threw the glass pipe and it shattered against the wall.

"That's old, Cortez. I don't mess with that stuff no more, I told you I gave that shit up." Joselyn lied.

"No… NO! You're not even supposed to have my kids. These are my kids and you got them around this bullshit. My son out here getting jumped in these streets defending your crackhead ass while these little niggas is teasing him about the grimy shit you're doing to get high. You're supposed to be protecting them, not the other way around!" Pops continued to yell at her.

Joselyn mumbled something incoherently and then it sounded like she was crying.

"I'm finished with this shit. I'm tired of giving you the benefit of the fucking doubt only for you to piss that shit back my way. You ain't never gonna see your fucking kids!" Pops stormed out of her room and yelled at us. "I said for y'all to come on!"

We both jumped as we scurried to grab our book bags. Mom stumbled out of her bedroom after my father.

"You can't take my babies from me, Cortez!" she cried.

"Get some help, Joselyn. Otherwise, if all you wanna do is get high and be out in these streets, I'm not bringing these kids back around you. And I mean that shit," Pops told her. He closed the truck door behind us after we climbed inside and then jumped in the driver seat before speeding off.

"Daddy, did I drop the money you gave me yesterday in the back of the truck" Janaya asked.

"Shut up, Jah-Jah…" I said in a low voice.

"No, baby-girl," Pops told her.

"I told you I put it in my book bag," Janaya sneered at me.

"What's the problem, you lost your money?" asked Pops.

"I put it in my book bag when you gave it to me and Davion took the book bag upstairs in my room, but when we came back home, the money wasn't in there," Janaya told him. I hunched my shoulders once I saw the pissed off expression on Pops' face through the rearview mirror.

"Fucking bitch," I heard him mumble.

We drove the rest of the way home in silence. When we got there and put our things away, Pops made us some pancakes, scrambled eggs and sausages for breakfast. Meagan was already at work, so we spent the day hanging with him. He did his best to make us laugh and try to keep things as normal as he could. But I could tell that it bothered the hell out of him that I had been jumped defending Joselyn against the neighborhood kids slandering her name. It would be over four years before we saw Joselyn again…

Yani

2nd Quarter

The loud whistle blew as my coach called time out and my teammates and I went over to our bench to go over the next play the coach wanted us to run.

"Jones, you have four fouls, you've got to play smarter out there. We still have a whole quarter to play and the last thing we need is for you to foul out on some bullshit, you hear me?" my coach said to me as he gave me the evil eye.

I sucked my teeth and huffed after gulping down some Gatorade. "That's cause that nut-ass guard keep grabbing my shirt. Why he ain't getting fouled for that?!" I sneered.

"Ay, watch your mouth!" the coach shot back at me. I shook my head and crossed my arms over my chest.

At thirteen years old, I had developed a bit of a temper and was even referred to by Pops as a "hot-head". In my eyes, I just didn't have much patience for people's bullshit.

Hoop Dreams Deflated

Coach went over the plays that he wanted us to run and warned us against making reckless moves and ball hogging versus sharing the ball. He also stressed the importance of drawing the foul instead of committing them, looking at me as he said that. I kept my lips zipped knowing if I said anymore smart shit, he was going to take me out of the game. Some of the students from Gratz and Dobbins were at the game watching, and I needed as many minutes on the floor as possible so word could keep spreading on how good I was.

The whistle blew again and I tucked my jersey back inside of my ball shorts as we made our way back out onto the floor. There were six minutes left in the final quarter and we were only up by three points. I was running the point at the moment and couldn't wait to cross over my opponent who kept grabbing my jersey. I was plotting in my head how dope it would be if I made that corny-ass nigga fall.

While LeBron was still my hero, my Dad put me on to this cat that was also from Philly named Shawn Williams. He was playing overseas for Italy and I made it a point to not only follow his games over there, but I had taken interest in the many

Yani

YouTube videos that people had of him from his senior year of high-school all the way through college when he was a Hoya. It definitely gave me hope that I could make it out of the 'hood and do something great with my basketball skills.

Alright, the whistle was blown. The ball was inbounded before it was passed to me. I put my hand up to signal to my teammates what play we were about to run as I dribbled the ball down to our end of the field. Just as I suspected that cornball-ass nigga would, he posted up on me. Oh yeah, I'ma fuck his ankles up today, B.

I faked to the left before dribbling the ball between my legs and then did a behind the back pass to a teammate who was wide open and made the jump shot. I threw my fist in the air and was about to back pedal down to the other end of the floor when the guy who was guarding me said some slick shit as he bumped me.

"I'ma let ya crack-baby-ass have that one. It's all good."

"Eat a dick, you pussy-ass bitch. Don't be salty cause y'all losing!" I snapped back at him.

Hoop Dreams Deflated

A whistle blew and the ref tee'd me up. I looked at him confused before throwing my hands up in the air. Was this nigga serious?

"A tech for what, man?!" I shouted at the ref.

My coach got up from the bench and it was obvious that he was pissed off at me.

"Jones, what the hell is going on?" the coach yelled at me.

"Nah man, this is bullshit. How I get a technical when bol' came out his mouth to me first. You ain't say shit to him! Fuck outta here with that dickhead shit, man!" I was pissed. The ref had been giving me grief for the whole game with bullshit calls. The whistle blew again and in a hyped manner, he signaled for me to be thrown out of the game.

My teammates grabbed me knowing that I had a hot temper and the assistant coach walked me off of the court as the crowd booed against the ref and his bullshit call. My team didn't have a chance without me on the floor. At least, that's how I saw it.

When I got into the locker room I kicked over a trashcan and punched my fist into a locker. It hurt like hell, but I was fucking hot. In the last few years, I had gotten into quite a few fights with guys for saying smart shit about my mother and her drug habit. I'd yet to lose a fight. You'd think with all of the ass whippings I had dished out, niggas would put those sneak shots to rest.

"You need to calm the hell down!" the assistant coach snapped at me.

I plopped down on a bench and put my hands to my face before resting my elbows on my knees.

"What the hell happened out there? How did you end up getting hit with a technical foul in the first-damn-place?" he asked me. I shook my head, refusing to look up at him.

"Look, you're good. There's no denying that. I've never coached anyone with as much talent, tenacity and determination as you. But your talent won't get you very far if you don't learn to control your anger, humble yourself and have a little self-control," he warned me.

I let out a deep sigh before leaning back on the bench and shaking my head. I had heard this speech far too many times and I wasn't in the mood for it today. I let him know that.

"My Pops been giving me the whole attitude is a little thing that makes a big difference speech since I was five years old. I'm really not in the mood for this right now." I snorted.

"Well you better get in the mood. Because one more ass-hole move like that and you're off the team. How long you think Coach is going to tolerate your shit, son?"

I frowned and huffed once more before crossing my arms over my chest. I didn't like the idea of being kicked off of the basketball team. Basketball was my life and one of the only things that kept me out of trouble. What kept me in trouble was constantly being picked on about the shit my mom was into.

"Now, I understand the situation with your mom and I sympathize with you, son. I truly do. But some things, as a child, are out of your control. Some battles are not meant for you to fight. You have to learn to ignore what you can't conquer, and conquer what you can't ignore," the assistant coach schooled.

Yani

I thought on his words for a moment which surprisingly, made sense. "I can't ignore the fact that my mom is being disrespected."

"So what, you're going to beat every nigga's ass that you feel as though is disrespecting you?" my coach shot back. "Not only is that not smart, but it's a sure, fire way to get your ass in more trouble than you can handle. Now, what if I told you that your mother is disrespecting herself?"

I looked over at my coach with cold eyes. His expression didn't change. As much as I wanted to hate Joselyn, she was my mother. After the first fight I had gotten into about her being disrespected, I understood why she was still a soft spot for Pops. We both saw the good in her, as well as her potential. All we wanted was for her to see that potential as well.

As though my coach had read my mind he said to me, "It's good that you want to defend your mother. That's a great thing. But at the same time, you have to understand that you can't help a person who doesn't want to be helped and doesn't have the got-damn common sense to help themselves."

"How do you know my mom doesn't want to be helped? Or that she doesn't want to help herself? Maybe she doesn't know how," I said back to him.

The coach sighed as he thought on my words. "You may very well be right, Davion. But again, you are just a child. There is only but so much that you can do to help. The biggest thing you can do is love her and show her that you love her. Knocking niggas out in the streets isn't helping her. Can't you see that?" he asked me.

I hunched my shoulders. "I guess so." I heard the final buzzer and looked towards the doors that the team would be coming in from wondering if we won the game or lost. Judging by how excited the team was when they came in, I was positive that we won.

"77-72!" One of my teammates shouted as he banged on the lockers. "Whose house?!" he yelled.

"Our house!" we yelled in return. I slapped each of my teammates hands as they passed by, telling them "good game". The coach stormed into the locker room, looking around. I saw the fire in his eyes when he finally located me. I knew I was in trouble.

Yani

"Jones!" he barked in a loud and intimidating voice.

"It's alright, Marshall. I talked to him. I think we're good, now. Right, Davion?" the assistant coach looked at me with his eye brows raised.

"Yes sir. We're good." I got up from the bench and went to my locker to retrieve my duffle bag. I didn't feel like showering there. I knew my dad and sister were outside in the car waiting for me and I would have to face the music from him, too.

"Good game, Dah-Dah!" Janaya said with a huge smile on her face when she saw me coming towards the car. Dad had upgraded to a banging onyx-black Chevy Silverado with chrome trimming, keyless entry, kick-ass surround sound and the bomb 24 inch rims. It was clean as hell and glistened in the early evening sun light. I gave my sister a high-five as I hopped inside of the truck.

"Hey Pop," I spoke before sneaking a peek at him to gauge how upset he was with me.

"Good game, son. But uh, what happened in that fourth quarter that got you thrown out of the game?" he asked me.

I sighed before fidgeting. "The ref wasn't being fair. He kept making BS calls against me for little stuff but wasn't calling nothing on the bol' that was guarding me, and I know he saw how the bol' was grabbing all on my jersey to try to keep me from getting passes."

"Okay…" my dad replied as though he was waiting for the rest of the story.

"Then the bol' said some ole slick stuff out of his mouth and I guess the ref heard what I said back and that's when he tee'd me up."

"What did the guy say to you?" My dad asked as he started the truck. The engine roared with authority and my dad turned the radio down as Meek Mill rapped about liking his Roze red and his diamonds blue. That was my jawn!

I hunched my shoulders and looked at the floor of the truck. "He called me a crack-baby."

"Mmm hmm, and what did you say back?"

I glanced at my father nervously. "I… I told him to eat a…" I trailed off before glancing at my father. He stared at me sternly. I knew I had no choice but to man up and answer his question. I shook my head, disappointed at myself and said, "I

Yani

told him to eat a dick and called him a pussy-ass-bitch and told him not to be salty because he was losing."

I could hear Janaya wince behind me in her seat. "Ooooh, Dah-Dah!" she squealed.

"Shut up, Janaya!" I snapped back at her.

"Quiet, both of you!" my father told us. He then turned to me. "When are you going to learn not to let the slick shit that these little knuckleheads say to you, get to you, huh?" my father asked me. He checked his side mirrors before pulling out and driving towards home.

"But dad…," I started to say.

"No buts, Davion. Why do you think they keep coming at your neck? Because you let them know that's your weakness and they're trying to get at you. You're making it easy for them. You gotta be smarter. Yeah it sucks that people know your momma was out there in those streets, but it is what it is. He said that slick shit to you and you played right into his hand. They know you a hot head and they did that shit hoping you would get pulled out the game figuring the team would lose without you. They salty because y'all still won, but what if y'all didn't? You gotta let that shit go." Pops schooled me. We stopped at a red light as I thought on Pops' words. He was always kicking game to me and I did my best to take his advice, but my temper was hard to control.

"Sorry, Dad." I mumbled.

"Don't apologize to me. Apologize to your team when you go to practice tomorrow and apologize to your coaches. And pick your head up. While I ain't too thrilled that you keep getting into dumb shit, you have nothing to be ashamed of. You're human."

I sat a moment longer with my head low before I leaned back and looked out the window. For some reason, my eyes became teary. I tried to discreetly wipe them away before my dad could see them falling but he knew. He placed his large hand over my head.

"It's okay, son. I understand," he said to me in a low voice. He turned the radio up as Trey Songs came on the radio. I sniffed as I wiped my face. I hated the effect my mother and her fucked up decisions had on me.

Pops swung over to our house in Cedarbrook and told me to get showered and changed so we

Yani

could all go out to dinner. He and Meagan were still together and he told us that he had a surprise for us.

After showering and getting dressed in a pair of True Religion Jeans and plain Polo shirt with a pair of Jordans, I began brushing my hair when I heard a knock at my door.

"Yo!" I replied as I brushed my waves. I was looking more and more like my dad every day.

Janaya opened my door. "You coming to my game Friday?" she asked me. My little sister was doing her thing on the basketball court also. Sometimes the guys tried to blow her off figuring a girl couldn't get down, but she had a mean jump-shot and her ball handling skills were just as good as mine. And even though she enjoyed playing basketball, there was nothing tom-boyish about her. She still liked wearing lip-gloss and got her nails done with Meagan at the shop. I could tell I was going to have to keep an eye on her when she became a teenager.

"Of course, I am. Why wouldn't I?"

Janaya hunched her shoulders as she walked over to my dresser. She fished through my tray and grabbed a wrist watch out before putting it on.

"You drawling, yo. You know I hate when you wear my stuff," I said to her as I brushed my hair some more.

"Your watches are way cooler than mine. Dad bought some lame Hannah Montana jawn. I don't even watch that show anymore. It sucks," she said as she rolled her eyes.

"Then tell him, not me. Put my watch back."

"Now you suck," she sneered as she rolled her eyes again. She placed my watch back and then let out an exaggerated sigh. That's when I knew she came into my room for something more than to brody my watch.

"What is it?"

"Well…" she hesitated. "I think I know what the surprise is that Pops said he had for us."

"Run it," I said to her as I checked my appearance out before sitting my brush back on my dresser. I turned to face her.

"I heard Pops talking to Meagan. I think mom called him or sent him a letter or something asking if she could start seeing us again…"

I cut my sister off as I shook my head. "Fuck that," I hissed.

Yani

"You didn't let me finish!" Janaya said anxiously.

"I don't need to," I said in return.

"Davion, listen!" Janaya said as she pulled on my shirt. I huffed as I looked down at her. After all these years, Janaya still had this fantasy in her head that mom was going to be a real-life Claire Huxtable and turn from crackhead to mom of the decade. One day she was going to have to wake the fuck up.

"What?" I said through clenched teeth.

"She stopped getting high. She's been clean for two years and has a job working at Hahnemann hospital doing clerical work or something. She just wants to see us and start spending time with us," Janaya said quickly. I swear, that girl was like the got-dam news. She could soak up gossip like a sponge would soak up water.

I looked down at her feeling skeptical. "What did Pops say?"

"He thinks we should give it a chance but Meagan is against it," Janaya told me.

"At least one of them is smart. I'm with Meagan on this one."

"Well, I want to see her."

Hoop Dreams Deflated

I turned towards my sister after heading to my bedroom door, looking at her as though she was crazy. "For what?"

Janaya looked down at the floor and hunched her shoulders. "I dunno. I just miss her, I guess."

"Your memory must be fucked. Do you not remember all the times she left us in the house to get high? How many times she left us in there hungry as shit with no food while she went out to get high, huh? How many times did Dad give you money or me money only for her to steal the shit so she could get high? You don't remember that? I got jumped because of her! Or did you forget!"

"But dad said when a person is trying, you don't bring up their past and throw it in their face. Let them try. She's trying, Dah-Dah!" Janaya argued back.

"Man, fuck that and fuck her. You go see her. I never wanna see her again," I hissed.

"Then why were you crying in the car earlier?" Janaya asked softly. We stared at each other for a moment. A part of me was angry that she pulled my card. Instead of responding, I left the room and went downstairs.

Yani

"You guys ready to go?" Pops asked. Janaya sulked down the stairs behind me.

"Yeah," we both mumbled.

Pops looked us both over and then looked at Meagan. She shrugged her shoulders unsure of what our problem was.

"Y'all good?" Pops asked us as he looked us over.

"Yeah," I mumbled. Janaya remained quiet. Pops studied us for a little longer and then sat his keys on the dining room table.

"I don't know what's up with you two, but we ain't leaving until it's worked out and settled. So, one of y'all better start talking," he said to us sternly.

We both remained silent for a minute, so to show us that he wasn't playing, my dad pulled the chair out from the table and sat down.

I sighed and blurted out, "Janaya was eaves dropping again!"

Janaya looked at me with wide eyes. "No, I wasn't!" she snapped back.

"Eaves dropping about what?" he asked.

"She said she heard you and Meagan talking and the surprise is that mom stopped getting high and wants to see us," I said quickly.

Dad shot his eyes at Janaya and she coward in the corner. "What did I tell you about listening in on grown folks' conversation? Didn't I tell you that's rude and a fast way to get bad information?"

"Yes, daddy." Janaya answered him. "But daddy, I did hear you say that and the only reason I said something to Davion is because I was excited about it. I want to see mom, but he doesn't. He keeps bringing up all the bad things that happened when we were younger and I told him that you said we can't always throw a person's mistakes in their face if they're trying. And mom is trying… isn't she?" Janaya asked. Her voice cracked at the end of her statement as though she was going to cry.

My father sighed. "Yeah, you're absolutely right. But sometimes it's not always that easy to overlook the wrongs that somebody has done, especially if it's been a pattern with them. When people show you who they are, you should believe them. Otherwise, you'll constantly keep opening the door for them to hurt you."

Yani

"Does that mean we can't see her?" Janaya sniffed before wiping her face.

Dad sighed again. "I don't know, baby-girl. When folks mess up the way your mother did, they have to earn back their trust and show that they are capable of being a good person. Now from what she said, she isn't doing drugs anymore and she has a job. But that's what she says. She needs to show that she's clean and is stable. Once she does and if you guys want to, then you can go see her."

"I don't want to see her," I said quickly with venom dripping from my words. The hate I had for her could be seen in my face and heard when I spoke.

"Davion, come on, man!" Janaya cried. She plopped down on the steps and covered her face as she cried.

"Man whatever. I've been saying since I was five that I didn't want to see that lady and nobody listened. Y'all told me I was a kid and I had to go."

"And you're still a kid," Dad said as he glared at me.

"But don't I have a say? The courts said I can refuse to see her at ten. I'm thirteen, now. I don't want to see her!" That was the first time I had raised my voice at my father but I needed him to hear me for once on this situation. And if it meant I got my ass whipped, so be it. But I wasn't going to that bitch's house, I didn't give a fuck how clean she said she was.

My father stared at me for a moment as Janaya continued to cry on the steps. I was shocked that he didn't get up and back slap the piss out of me. He then looked at Janaya and then looked at Meagan.

"Please, Davion. Can you just go once? I don't want to go without you. But I want to see mom." Janaya said in a trembling voice.

I looked back at her and could tell that she was broken up. Meagan had been good to us over the last seven years and I couldn't help but wonder if she felt slightly betrayed.

Janaya's sad, big brown eyes killed me inside. I shook my head and sighed before sitting next to her on the steps. My love for my baby sister was greater than my hate for our mother.

"Okay, Jah-Jah. I'll go. Stop crying. I'll go with you." I said to her as I put my arm around her and

Yani pulled her close. She began to calm down after a moment.

Pops stood up and grabbed his keys. "Go wash your face so we can still go to dinner. Y'all good on Outback Steakhouse?" he asked us.

"Yesssss!" Janaya jumped up feeling rejuvenated. She ran upstairs to wash her face while Dad, Meagan and I went out to the truck. My Pops placed his hand on the top of my head and pulled me close to him.

"This means a lot to your sister. Try to understand that even though she has some of the same memories as you, in her eyes, y'all mom is like God to her."

"If you say so," I mumbled before climbing in the truck. I was silent for the ride to the restaurant and for the duration of dinner. In fact, I barely touched my food because I had lost my appetite. Janaya, Dad and Meagan talked endlessly, sharing jokes and laughing, having a good ole time. I felt like I didn't belong there and wanted to hurry up and go back home so I could lock myself inside of my room.

After seeing that I had no intentions of interacting with any of them, Pops signaled the waiter and asked for a to go tray for my food. He looked disappointed in me, but if only he understood how betrayed I felt. Mom was unfit in my eyes, point blank period. The courts deemed her unfit and had Dad not come and rescued us when he did, DHS probably would have stepped in and deemed her unfit. How is it that everyone could see this shit, including Meagan, who wasn't even our real mother, except Pops and Janaya. Yeah, I wanted to hurry up and go the hell home. There was nothing to smile, joke or laugh about that night.

As soon as we got home, I went up to my room, closed my door and turned out the lights. I then turned on my lava lamp. Even though I was thirteen and most of the stuff in my room had been updated as I matured and began liking new things, the one thing that remained the same was the lava lamp. I stared intently at the ceiling as the lit up dinos moved about before sighing deeply. I had a lot of woo-sahing to do before heading to my mother's tomorrow. Before I knew it, I had fallen fast asleep…

The next morning, Janaya was too happy. I woke up to her listening to her mixed CD with

Beyoncé yelling about girls running the world. I hated that singer. I swear I never saw what the hype was about with her. Any half naked chick with an ass can hop around the stage like they were possessed. Stand in front of a mic and bellow out a song like Whitney Houston or Patti LaBelle and move the crowd with your voice alone and then I'll be impressed. Until then, I'll pass.

I showered and dressed and packed up a couple changes of clothes along with my basketball. At the last minute, I decided to grab my PSP Vista so I would have something to do to occupy my time. I wasn't hanging with Lamar anymore and I didn't care for too many of those niggas from the block, so unfortunately, I would be spending time in the house.

"Y'all come on so I can drop y'all off. I have some errands I need to run also!" Dad yelled at us from downstairs. I tried to put on a poker face to mask how annoyed and pissed off I was that I was going to hell, but I don't think Pops was buying it. He looked at my face and shook his head. I was surprised that he didn't give me one of his father/son speeches.

Hoop Dreams Deflated

Janaya was way too happy to be going. She bopped down the steps with her distressed jeans, high top Adidas and grey Lady Chiefs team sweat shirt on with her hair pulled back into a ponytail that dangled on the back of her neck. As usual, her face glistened with cocoa butter and her lips held a glossy look. The first boy I caught looking at her for more than five seconds, I was going to knock his ass smooth…

"Davion? You don't hear me talking to you?" My father said, snapping me out of my thoughts.

"No sir. Sorry, I guess I was thinking too hard," I replied in a low tone.

My dad peered at me for a moment and began walking to the front door. We followed behind him.

"Make sure you look after your sister and try not to give your mom a hard time…"

"Yeah, I know. Because attitude is a little thing that makes a big difference," I said flatly. My father stopped at the door and turned to look at me. He shook his finger at me before shaking his head and opened the front door.

"Boy… your mouth," he said as we headed to his truck.

Yani

I imagined that I was skating on thin ice and didn't want to try my luck so I kept my mouth closed.

We hopped in his truck and then sped off to my mother's block. It had been more than three years since I had been around there, and some shit just doesn't change. Niggas was still hanging on the corner bullshitting. Fast-ass girls were still in their faces trying to bag the flyest catch. The entire scene disgusted me. I vowed that if I ever had kids, I would not have kids with a chick from a fucked up neighborhood like this, and I would never let my kids live in a fucked up environment like this. Maybe that's what Pops meant when he said he wanted me to make better choices than he did and be a better man than him.

I was a bit shocked when we parked in front of Joselyn's door and saw where she touched up the place. She had a new screen door as well as a new front door. The front was neat and had different colored flowers planted that made the place more cheerful. Maybe she really was making a change for the better.

Joselyn came to the door and looked better than she did the last time we saw her. She had gained a bit of weight and wasn't as skinny and frail as she was the last time we were there. Her hair was done nicely in what the chicks called a Bob, and her skin glowed. She didn't look anything like her previous drug abusing self. I was beginning to feel better about the situation.

After hugging Daddy as usual and making the fart noises on each other's cheeks, Janaya ran over to Joselyn and gave her a big hug. I got out of the truck apprehensively. Unless my eyes were deceiving me, I think Joselyn was crying as she was holding Janaya.

"Remember what I said, Davion," my father said to me sternly.

I nodded my head. "I know, Pops. Everybody deserves a second chance." He tapped my fist in midair and I fixed the strap to my duffle bag over my shoulder before walking over to Joselyn slowly.

"Oh, my baby boy! Look at how tall you've gotten!" she squealed before bursting into tears. She hugged me tightly as she cried, kissing my cheeks and squeezing me. She then pulled Janaya over to us and we shared a big three-way hug. After a moment, she let us go and wiped her face before

Yani

looking over at our father. "Thank you," she said through her tears.

I looked at my father and saw him nod in return. "You good?" he asked her.

"Yes. Everything straight with you?" she asked him back.

"As well as can be expected. Call me if they need anything. I'll be back Friday to get Janaya to take her to her game." Joselyn nodded her head and then brought us in the house.

I would be lying if I said I wasn't impressed with the transformation she put the house through. The dirty carpet in the house was gone and replaced with cherry colored hard-wood floors. There were mirrors on the wall and the old furniture was replaced with a new tanned colored leather sectional. It looked much brighter than the last time we were here. My facial expression didn't show how slightly impressed I was, though. The house might look different, but was she any different?

"Do you guys wanna put your bags upstairs in your rooms and then come down for something to eat?" Joselyn asked us.

"Sure!" Janaya said happily.

Hoop Dreams Deflated

"I'm not hungry," I replied blandly. I went upstairs and went into my room. I saw where she tried to hook it up in a way that she thought would make me happy but again, I wasn't impressed. I dropped my duffle bag down in the middle of the floor and plopped down on the small twin-sized bed. I would've much rather been at home.

Janaya could be heard bolting down the stairs loudly. I listened to the excitement in her voice as she filled her mother in on school, being on the honor roll, knowing how to draw, playing basketball and other things. She was much more excited to be talking to Joselyn than I was. How soon people forget.

I got up from my bed and went downstairs. Standing in the corner with my arms folded across my chest, I chose to listen to Janaya and Joselyn's conversation rather than join in. As far as I was concerned, there was nothing to talk about. Finally, Joselyn looked up at me.

"Davion, how come you're so quiet?" she asked me.

I hunched my shoulders, "I don't feel like talking. Can I get something to drink?"

Yani

"Sure," Joselyn told me as she pointed to the fridge. "There are some bottles of Arizona in there and a case of Poland Spring water in the corner.

I nodded my head, still refusing to say much before grabbing a bottle of Arizona from the fridge. At least she actually had some food in there that wasn't beyond the expiration date.

I cracked it open and took a sip as Joselyn and Janaya continued their girly chatter, which was starting to get on my damn nerves. If only Lamar hadn't been a dick-head, I would have rolled out and gone to his crib. At that moment, I wondered how Ms. Aretha was doing.

"Does Ms. Aretha still live around the corner?" I asked.

"Yeah why, are you going to hang out with Lamar?" Joselyn asked.

"Nah, I just wanted to say hi," I walked out of the house without asking for permission. As far as I was concerned, I didn't need it.

I walked through the neighborhood not paying any of the people out there any mind. As I raised my hand to knock on Ms. Aretha's door once I had arrived, she opened it. We both jumped.

"Davion?!" she exclaimed. She grabbed me and hugged me tightly. I hadn't seen her since the day her son let me get jumped on our way home from the store. "Oh my God, baby! How have you been? Look at how tall you've gotten!"

I smiled. "I've been good, Ms. Aretha. How are you?"

"I'm hanging in there. Where's your sister?"

"She's with my mom," I told her. Ms. Aretha nodded her head. She looked like she wanted to say something but was choosing her words wisely as though she didn't want to upset me.

"She looks like she's been doing much better lately," she finally said. I shrugged my shoulders not wanting to respond one way or another. She showed me into the house and closed the door behind us. I happened to look up at the stairs and saw Lamar standing in the middle of the landing, looking down at us.

"What's up, Lamar?" I spoke. Shockingly I wasn't as pissed as I thought I would have been when I saw him. I guess I was maturing a little.

Lamar smiled. "Hey… Dah-Dah." He came down the steps and gave me a strong handshake before we hugged each other. He had grown just as much as me but was a little taller. Despite what happened three years before, he was still my homeboy. Ms. Aretha smiled at our reunion. It was like we'd never missed a beat and the bond we shared as bloodless brothers had never been broken. We immediately began talking about basketball, the latest video games, and our favorite anime show, Naruto. Ms. Aretha went into the kitchen and began cooking as Lamar took out the controllers to his PS3 so we could begin playing Call of Duty.

That night, we filled our bellies with Ms. Aretha's dirty rice, fried chicken breasts and string beans. While Meagan was a pretty good cook, I had never come across anyone who could cook as well as Ms. Aretha.

Lamar and I continued playing video games until it was after 11pm when I heard a knock at the door. Lamar paused the game and got up to peek out of the peep hole.

"Oh shit, it's your mom," Lamar whispered.

I shook my head, rolled my eyes and waved her off. Lamar opened the door.

"How you doing, Ms. Joselyn?" Lamar spoke after opening the door for her.

"Hi, Lamar. Is Davion still here?" I heard her ask. I continued playing the game as though she wasn't there.

"Yes, ma'am. You can come in." Lamar stepped back so Joselyn could come inside.

"Boy, do you know what time it is?" Joselyn asked in a stern voice.

I continued playing the game and said to her in a dismissive manner, "Yeah, I'll be home when I'm done."

"Um, no. That's not how it works. I don't know what you do at your father's house but I'm sure staying out until after 11 o'clock isn't one of them. I shouldn't even have to come out here to look for you. Let's go. Now."

"Yeah, you don't know. And ain't nobody tell you to come around here to get me. I've been finding my way home just fine since I was six. I know how to get there," I sneered back at her as I continued playing the game. I was getting hot. Who the hell did she think she was, trying to play the mommy role. Bitch must be tripping.

Yani

I felt her snatch me by my arm and pull me up. "Boy, get your ass up, who the hell do you think you're talking to like that?!" she hissed back at me.

I snatched away from her. "Get off me, man!" I shot back at her.

"Davion!" I heard Ms. Aretha shout at me. "You better check yourself. Now, as long as I've been allowing you to come in my house, I've never seen this disrespectful side to you, but I'm not going to stand for it and I'm certainly not going to stand to see you disrespect your mother like this, especially in my house. It's late. Go on home and you can come back when your attitude is better."

I looked at Ms. Aretha for a moment biting my tongue extra hard and reminding myself that she was not the problem; Joselyn was. I then looked at Lamar who appeared nervous as hell at the moment. Then I shot a cold look at *her* before pushing past her and storming out of the house.

"I'm sorry, Joselyn. I went upstairs to fold up the laundry and only meant to lay down for a few minutes because I was so tired. Had I known it was this late, I would have had Lamar walk him home sooner." Ms. Aretha apologized.

"It's okay. Thank you, Ms. Aretha." Joselyn said nervously. "Good night, Lamar."

Lamar waved to her and Joselyn left out of the house. I was already half-way up the block.

"Davion, you better wait a damn minute!" I heard her call after me. I continued walking angrily up the street, ignoring her. She'd better get the fuck out of my face.

She ran to catch up to me. "What the hell was that back there, huh?" she asked me. I ignored her as I kept walking. "Davion," she said before grabbing my shirt to stop me.

"Yo man, stop grabbing my clothes." I snapped as I yanked away from her. I stormed up the steps to the porch and pushed the door open. I was heading upstairs when I heard her behind me.

"Ot'ine, bring your little ass back down these damn steps!"

"And what'chu gonna do… beat me?" I remarked smartly with a smirk on my face.

"I don't have to lay a finger on you. I can just call your dad to let him know how disrespectful you're being and I'm sure he'll drive over here tonight and tap dat ass!" Joselyn said as she stormed over to me and got in my face. I stared at her for a moment and then shrugged my shoulders as though I didn't care. A part of me did, but I didn't want her to know that. She looked taken aback by my lack of giving a fuck about her threat. She then closed her eyes and sighed.

"Davion… I know you are probably still upset about how things were when you were a child, but believe me, baby, I did my best…"

I cut her off at those words. "Your best? That's what you call your best? Leaving us in this dirty house with no food while you ran out getting high was your best?" I shot back at her.

Joselyn's eyes became teary. "You have no idea what I was going through back then. None! It may look like it was easy for me to just…" she stopped as she became choked up and put her hands to her face.

"I got jumped defending you. I get into fights almost every week because niggas out here in the streets forever coming at my neck, calling me a crack-baby and calling you a whore, talking about you sucking dick for dime bags of blow! That's the result of you doing your best, Joselyn. If it wasn't for Pops…"

"What!" Joselyn yelled at me. "If it wasn't for your dad, I wouldn't have been strung out in the first got-damn place." Things became mad quiet when those words hit the walls of the house. The silence was so damn thick you could slice through it with a steak knife. I could hear my heartbeat in my eyes as I stared at Joselyn making sure I heard her correctly. "Yeah, I bet he never told you that shit. Who do you think gave me my first high, huh? He did. But he won't tell you that shit. He won't tell you how he laced my weed with cocaine so I would be relaxed enough for him to try anal on me. He won't tell you how his way of thanking me for letting him sell drugs out of this house after I had you was to throw me a couple hundred dollars and some coke. *Thanks bae…*" she mocked him in a hateful tone. "Only for him to leave me after I had Janaya for that yellow bitch y'all have more respect for than me. That was my payback for being his ride or die chick."

My eyes stung with tears as I listened to what she said but I didn't want to believe it. I waved my hand at her in a dismissive manner before turning

Yani

to my bedroom door. I didn't even remember walking up the stairs.

"Whatever, man. You always trying to blame somebody for your problems. You ain't never going to change. My dad ain't never do that to you. You's a liar, a thief, and a crack-whore! Stick to the script. Don't try to change it now. Tryna' be a mom. Get your crackhead-ass outta here." I went in my room and slammed my door in her face.

I was hot. Oh, I was mad pissed. I kept hearing what she said about my father being the one to get her strung out on drugs echoing in my head. I sat on the bed for a moment with both fists to my face, rocking back and forth, trying to calm down but it wasn't working. I bolted upward and paced rapidly across my floor back and forth breathing heavy, trying my best not to let the tears fall, but they broke through the dam of my eye lids and fell down my cheeks, which only pissed me off even more. I kicked my dresser before sliding to the floor on my knees and balled my eyes out. Everybody had lied to me. All my life…

The next morning, I got up extra early, hoping to get out of the house before Joselyn woke up. I didn't want to run into her after what was said the night before. I noticed that her bed was made and she wasn't in it. The house was also quiet. Good, maybe she'd left early to go to work.

I showered and got dressed quickly before waking Janaya up so she could do the same. We then ate some Toaster's Strudels before washing them down with a few Capri Sun juices. I threw a few more in my duffle bag so we would have something to drink while we were out.

As we headed over to the Recreation Center, I noticed how quiet Janaya had been all morning. I then wondered if she heard the argument between me and Joselyn the night before. I wanted to ask her, but wasn't sure how I was going to explain mom's accusations. So instead, I opted to keep my mouth closed.

"What's wrong?" I finally asked Janaya as we were getting ready to run some drills on the basketball courts.

Janaya shook her head. "Nothing. My stomach just hurts."

Yani

"You wanna sit out for a little bit to see if you feel better and then play some ball?" I asked her as I tied the strings to my ball sneaks.

Janaya shook her head. "Nah, I'm good." We went out on the courts and began running drills, practicing our dribbling with two balls as well as dribbling between our legs. We then practiced free throw shooting and jump shots before we played a few one on one games. At the end of the last game, Janaya leaned on her knees wincing.

"You sure you're okay?" I asked her again.

"Yeah, let me run to the bathroom," she said in return.

"Alright. You wanna run another game or go get something to eat?"

"Can we get something to eat and then go back to the house?"

I wasn't ready to go back to the house so soon or at all, as a matter of fact. I nodded my head and finished packing up my duffle bag as Janaya made her way back to the bathroom. A few moments later, she was hurrying out with an awkward look on her face as though something was wrong. She hurried over to me.

"I need to go home. Like, right now," she said quickly.

"What's the problem?" I asked with a frown.

"There's blood in my underwear and I don't know where it's coming from. I tried to wipe it off but it wouldn't stop so I just put a bunch of tissue in my pan…"

"Wooaaah!" I said, cutting my sister off. "Um… ok…" I stammered, not knowing what to say. I mean for Christ's sake, I'm a thirteen-year-old boy. What the hell am I supposed to tell my sister about getting her period for the first time? And why the hell is she getting her period at ten-fucking-years-old anyway?! "Ok… just calm down Jah-Jah. It sounds like you got your period. Let's go home and if mommy is there, she can show you what to do."

"What if she isn't?" Janaya asked in a frightened tone. I shuttered at the thought of having to show my sister how to use a pad or a tampon.

"We'll worry about that when we get there. Turn around." I told her. I checked her shorts and noticed that she had blood on them. I cursed under my breath as I thought of what to do. I then snatched my shirt from over my head and told her to put it on. When she did, I checked her again to make sure it covered the back of her shorts. The last thing I needed was to have to beat somebody's ass because their immature ass wanted to tease her for getting her period. We then hurried home.

"Alright, if mommy isn't here, just look in the medicine cabinet and get the jawns that says *Always with Wings*. Take a shower, too." I said to my sister. She ran in the house as I sat on the steps rolling my basketball between my legs while I waited for her. A few moments later, Janaya ran back out of the house.

"Davion!" she screamed.

"What?" I asked, becoming annoyed.

"Mom is on the couch and she won't get up. I can't wake her up and she's not moving!" she told me as she was trembling.

"What?" I scrambled to my feet and ran in the house. I'll never forget this day as long as I live. Every single detail will stay with me, remaining vivid as though it had just happened no matter how much time goes by.

Hoop Dreams Deflated

Joselyn was stretched out on the couch appearing as though she was asleep. She was dressed in a pretty, light-pink colored pair of slacks and a cream blouse. Her make-up looked fresh and her eyes were closed as though she was sleeping. But something inside of me told me that that wasn't the case.

"Joselyn, get up." I said as I shook her. She didn't wake up. "Joselyn," I said louder before slapping her face. She still didn't move. Fear washed over my body as I began to tremble. I tried to convince myself that she was just in a deep sleep, but the needle in her left arm told me otherwise.

"No mommy… no!" I whined. "Mom, get up! Get up, mom! GET UP!" I said as loud as I could. I could hear Janaya crying for her behind me, also telling her to get up but I knew that she wouldn't. Fear, guilt and sorrow was all that I felt as I grabbed onto her and buried my face in her chest. Even though she was very still, she still felt very warm. I cried for my mom and begged God to make it not so because I needed to tell her I was sorry and take back the things that I said the night before.

Yani

I didn't even hear Janaya when she left the house, but she came back in with a man that I wasn't familiar with.

"Son, I need you to step back for me please, so I can try to help your mother," the man said to me.

I was too choked up to bother asking him who the hell he was. I moved out of his way and watched as he laid her completely flat on the sofa. He checked her wrist and then placed two fingers on her neck. He then listened close to her mouth for a moment.

"Is she… is she dead?" I asked as I hugged Janaya close to me. She was balling her eyes out. The man looked at me and then looked at Janaya before nodding his head sorrowfully. He then pulled out his cell phone and everything else after that was a blur. I barely remember the coroner putting her body in a body bag and taking her out of the house nor do I remember when my father got there. His eyes were red as though he had been crying for the entire ride over to us. He wrapped his arms around both of us and pulled us close. I was numb, extremely numb. I called my mother a crack-whore the night before and even worse, told her she would never be a good mother. Did I cause her to go out and shoot a deadly hit in her arms that cost her her life? Was it because I did exactly what my father always told me not to do, which was throw a person's past in their face when they were trying to change for the better? Had I done this? Or was it his fault for getting her started on that shit to begin with?

The next few days were the hardest of my life. Janaya slept in my room again for the first time in over three years. While she cried almost all day and all night, I remained quiet out of guilt. I partially believed I was to blame for my mother taking that deadly hit. But even as I blamed myself, my need to question Pops about what Joselyn said the night before she died grew stronger with that guilt.

I sat in the middle of the stairs as Pops was talking to a woman, going over the funeral arrangements for Joselyn. I took a page from Janaya's book and decided to do a little ear hustling. From what I heard, Joselyn didn't have a life insurance policy, so dad was paying for her funeral out of his own pockets. Her mother and father were dead which is how she got the house on

Yani

Medary street. Though she didn't have any life insurance, she did have a will and left me and Janaya the house.

The woman helped pops write out the obituary for Joselyn. I don't know when he did it, but he managed to get some pretty decent pictures of her from her Facebook page. When it was all done, I heard Pops ask the woman how much he owed her.

"Okay, the family car, tombstone, service and funeral home expenses along with the obituary layout and copies will be…" she tapped a few keys on her iPhone, "Twelve thousand, eight hundred forty-seven dollars and ninety-seven cents."

I mouthed "Got-damn," and wondered where the hell Pops was going to come up with that kind of money to pay this woman. I watched from where I was sitting as Pops stood up and went over to what I thought was an ordinary painting on the wall. He pressed something on the side and it opened like a mini door. Behind it was a safe. He quickly put the combination in, reached inside and counted out the money he needed before handing it to the woman. She thumbed through it before tucking it in her brief case. I wondered to myself where the hell Pops got that kind of money. I never bothered to question what kind of work he did. But after hearing what Joselyn said before she died and seeing the stack of cash he gave to the woman, I began to wonder even more.

Pops walked the lady to the door after thanking her for her services and then closed and locked up when she left. I came all the way down the stairs as though I had not heard or seen anything. But I had questions and it was time for him to start giving up answers.

"How you doing, son?" Pops asked me as he pushed the chairs back to the table. I shrugged my shoulders without saying anything and stood over by the wall to our dining room. I was trying to figure out how I was going to start this conversation off.

"Have you eaten anything?"

I shook my head. "No, I'm not really hungry."

Pops sighed. "Davion, you gotta eat something. I know you're hurting, but if you don't eat anything, you're going to get sick. Where's your sister?"

"She's upstairs in her room laying down."

Pops was silent for a moment and then went into the kitchen. "I'm about to make me a sandwich. I want you to eat one, too. Even if you don't eat the whole thing, just try to eat some of it."

I sulked as I made my way into the kitchen behind him and sat at the counter. I didn't want a damn sandwich. I wanted to know if what my mother said was true and he was the one who got her strung out on drugs before leaving her assed out, and addicted to crack and heroin before starting a better life with Meagan.

"You look like you have something on your mind, Davion. You wanna talk?" Pops asked me, snapping me out of my thoughts.

"No, I'm not really in the mood to talk," I mumbled.

Pops peered at me with a look of sympathy on his face. He took everything he needed to make our sandwiches out of the refrigerator as well as some beverages. As he began making lunch for us both, he started giving me the usual father-son heart to heart talk. I didn't hear what he was saying, though. I could hear his voice, but he sounded as though he was far away, while over his voice I could hear my mother.

"I bet he never told you that shit. Who do you think gave me my first high, huh? He did…"

"How come you never told us you were the one who started getting mom high?" I blurted out.

Dad froze in the middle of spreading Miracle Whip across a piece of potato bread. It suddenly became mad quiet in the kitchen as I looked at him trembling.

"This is a test of the emergency broadcast system…" is what I heard before that flat lining beeping sound. Pops sat the butter knife down on the table and I was positive he was about to slap the shit out of me.

"Who told you that? Huh? Did your mother tell you that?" Pops asked me.

I swallowed past a lump of fear in my throat. "Is it true?" I asked back.

If looks could kill, I would have been joining Joselyn to sing a duet for Saint Peter from the way Pops glared at me. I saw the twitch in his jaw and knew I was in trouble.

"Your mother's biggest problem was her lack of accountability. She always wanted to blame everyone else for her problems instead of taking responsibility for them."

I smirked and shook my head. "Mom said you sold drugs out of her house and would toss her a couple hundred and some coke before you thanked her. And then you left her for Meagan. You left us in that house knowing mom had a coke habit because of you! You left us and bought this bomb house with Meagan and lived well while we were starving!" I said with my voice cracking while I tried not to cry.

Pops was quicker than I imagined. He reached across the counter and slapped the dog shit out of me. I almost fell from the stool but clung to the side of the counter to hold myself up. He came around the counter and snatched me up by my collar.

"Before you go running your mouth about shit, make sure you have all the damn facts. You don't question me about a muthafucking thing when I'm the one feeding you, clothing you, and keeping a got-damn roof over your muthafucking head! I left y'all and came and lived well!? Boy!" my father snarled as he jerked me. He let me go with a shove, breathing heavily.

"Your mother's coke habit is the reason I left her. She almost cost me my got-damn life stealing my money and getting into shit. The only reason I didn't take you and your sister with me is because I was living out of suit cases in an apartment with four other niggas living in that muthafucker. Where the fuck was y'all going to sleep? I heard the rumors about your mom, but I ain't wanna believe the shit no more than you or Janaya did. Soon as I got my shit together and had a stable place, I came for y'all and I fought my ass off to make sure I got y'all LEGALLY!"

Pops looked hurt as he talked to me. But he still didn't confirm or deny that he was the one who got my mom started on drugs.

"So, you weren't the one who laced her weed with cocaine so she would be more relaxed for y'all to have sex?" I asked him looking him straight in the eye.

Pops looked at me for a moment and then looked away without saying anything. It was the first time in all of my life that I saw him as less than a man. To not answer me was an admission of guilt. He bad mouthed my mother like she wasn't shit for all of those years when it was his fault that she was the way she was and ultimately died the way she did. I wondered if it ever occurred to him that maybe her addiction was because of how he left her after she trusted him to never do her dirty.

I got up from the counter and went up to my room. I picked up my cell phone from off of my dresser and opened my Facebook page. Not long ago, Joselyn had sent me a friend request but I had never accepted it. I clicked on her page and went to her pictures. She had so many pictures of me and Janaya when we were little. She even had pictures of me from basketball games. It dawned on me that she was coming to my games and not saying anything, probably not wanting to run the risk of embarrassing me.

I enlarged her profile picture which was of her standing near her front door smiling. She looked happy and full of life. I touched her face as the tears stung my eyes. Even though it didn't matter, I accepted her friend request. I then burst into tears.

"I'm sorry, mom…" I choked in between sobs. I curled up in a ball on my bed and cried until my head and my heart hurt. I wanted my mom back. I wanted her back, but I couldn't have her and it hurt so damn bad…

The funeral was a blur. Janaya took it the hardest. She sat next to me throughout the service with her head resting on my shoulder. So many people from the neighborhood came to pay their respects, or to be nosey. It didn't really matter to me. They shook my father's hand as well as mine and gave Janaya a hug.

At the grave site, Janaya and I stood next to each other holding each other's hands. We squeezed each other's hand as our way of comforting one another and to help the other to remain strong. After laying the gold roses on her casket, they began descending Joselyn down into the ground. Janaya buried her face in the sleeve of my suit jacket and I laid my head against hers. But when Pops tried to put his arm around me to comfort us, I yanked away from him and walked back to the family limo. No way would I ever look at Pops the same way anymore…

HalfTime

*Th*ree more years had gone by. I was a Junior at Central High School and the star of the basketball team running the point. I had been the first freshman since Shawn Williams to start on a high school varsity team and lead the school to a championship. I had also been featured in numerous newspapers and even a few local sports magazines. Many had labeled me as someone to look out for. I had shot up in height to 6'4 and weighed 195lbs. While most of my close homies from when I was a young-buck still called me Dah-Dah, most people referred to me as *Ice Breaker* because I stayed fucking somebody's ankles up on the basketball courts.

Janaya still played basketball, too. Her game and ball handling skills had gotten crazy. She was a bit tall for a 13-year-old standing at 5'7. Though she still had a baby face, she unfortunately had the body of a grown woman, which is why I stuck to her like flies on shit. A couple times, I caught my friends checking her out and I almost had to fuck up one of my home-boy's fronts for trying to bag her while she was on her way home from school one day. I had a hunch to meet her at the bus-stop but was running late. She hated when I did that, insisting that she wasn't a baby anymore. So, I made it look like I'd just happened to be coming from the store around the time I knew her bus was pulling up. She was an 8th grader at Amy Northwest and I knew the H bus would be dropping her off soon.

"Ay Jah-Jah," my boy Chris said as he cracked a grin. My sister fixed her book-bag on her back as she peered at him.

"What's up, Chris?" she replied blandly.

"I'm chilling, you know. Staying out the way 'n shit. So, what's up wit'chu?" he asked as he rubbed his hands together.

"Nothing. About to knock this homework out real quick so I can hit the rec up with my brother."

"Yeah? That's what's up. So, look right, I be seein' you every day out here looking all cute 'n shit but you'on never gimme no holla."

"Okay…" my sister replied.

Yani

"So, I'm saying, what's up with me 'n you havin' a lil' Love and Basketball thing popping?"

"Naw, I'm good," my sister flee'd him. I wanted to laugh as I walked behind them.

"What, I'm ugly or something?" Chris asked her. I shook my head.

"Oh naw, you ain't ugly. I'm just not on that type time wit'chu."

"How come?" he pressed.

"First off, 'cause you my brother's mans. Second, 'cause you too old for me. If my brother don't fuck you up for that, Pops definitely gonna be on your top. And third, I really ain't trying to talk to no boys right now. I got other shit to worry about," my sister broke it down for him.

"*Yeah!*" I thought to myself. I was glad my sister wasn't like most of the fast-ass girls out here, but I had told her too many times to watch her mouth. I was trying to teach her she could be sassy with class. A foul mouth made chicks look trashy. I hated chicks that cursed like grown men. That shit was the bid.

"Come on, yo, you tryna' play me. I ain't that much older than you. Me and Davion the same age. And ain't nobody scared of your pops like that.

And Davion ain't trying to catch these hands either. He tall as shit, but I'll still knock that nigga the fuck out," he chuckled.

"How sway? Chris, you know I'll beat yo' ass up and down Michener street, don't play yourself." I said from behind them.

Janaya turned around and shook her head. "You following me again, Dah-Dah?"

"Yo, you a whole creep, nigga. How long you been behind us?" Chris asked, changing the subject.

"Long enough. Yo, stay away from my sister, bruh, seriously. She already told you she ain't checking for you. Keep that shit moving, yo."

"I was only joking wit' her. Chill out, cuz." Chris waved me off.

"Yeah, whatever. I ain't laughing and I don't play about my baby sis, either. She ain't no jawn. Stick with the hoodrat bitches you been sticking with." I said with base in my voice.

Chris backed down but stared at me with a smirk. He then slapped me a handshake. "Yeah, she like my lil' sis, too. I was just fucking with her. You coming to Simon's later?"

Yani

"Yeah I'll be around," I told him as me and Janaya started walking towards the house.

"Alright, my G." Chris turned to head towards his house and I looked at Janaya before shaking my head.

"What?" she asked.

"What I tell you about your mouth, man?" I scolded her as I took a sip from my Vitamin water.

She sucked her teeth before waving me off. "Man, niggas like Chris you can't be nice to when you blow them off. You gotta be gritty to let 'em know what's up. Otherwise, they keep pressing. I was just trying to stop him at the door."

I nodded my head, agreeing with her. "True. But you see that nigga was still pressin'."

"I can handle myself, Dah-Dah. You're not always gonna be lurking in the shadows."

I burst out laughing and then she laughed with me. "Yo, you make me sound like a weirdo when you say it like that."

"Because you are! You all creeping behind us while we're walking down the street. Like, who does that?" We both laughed again.

"Ay, I'm just looking out for you, making sure these niggas don't try no sucker shit."

"I know, bro. It's all good. I appreciate it," Janaya smiled as she stuffed her hands in her jacket pocket. "You still a weirdo, though." We laughed again.

"Whatever, man. How was school?"

"It was cool. The counselor told me I have an interview with Central next Wednesday at 10am. I might be in there next year with you."

"That's what's up. You got homework?"

"Yeah. I'm having trouble with this scientific notation stuff my math teacher gave me so, can you help me with it before you go play ball?" Janaya asked me as we got to the house.

I pulled my keys out. "Yeah, I got you."

We went inside the house and Janaya dropped her book bag on floor before heading straight to the kitchen. It was routine for her ever since she started school to raid the refrigerator after school and fix herself something to eat.

Meagan and Dad were now married. They tied the knot a year after Joselyn died. Our relationship wasn't as tight as it was when I was a kid, before learning he was the one who got mom started with using drugs. And even though he had managed to keep a tight lid on it for so many years, I learned that he was a major dope distributor but co-owned a supermarket, which is how he kept his money clean. The supermarket was primarily in Meagan's name along with a hair salon that she owned. He kept that business separate just in case anything happened.

Learning that about my Pops made me lose even more respect for him. He preached to me throughout my childhood the importance of being an honorable, trustworthy man when all this time he was nothing more than a dope dealer who used one woman to get his dirty business started and hides behind another woman to keep his business going. Where's the honor in that shit?

My phone went off with a text message. Pops had just gotten me the new iPhone 5s and an iPhone 5c for Janaya.

"Hey Dah-Dah," the text message said.

I didn't recognize the number so I texted back *"Who dis?"* I waited for a response.

"You funny. It's Tashai. Stop playing with me."

I smirked to myself. It was the chick I went to middle school with who I ran into while coming from getting a haircut over the weekend.

"What's up, Shorty?" I texted back.

"Dah-Dah, you know where Pops went?" Janaya asked me.

"Naw," I mumbled as I read Tashai's message. *"Come chill with me,"* her text message said.

"Where you live at?" I asked back. She texted back the address and made sure to tell me her mom had already left for work. It was a booty call.

"Yo, I'm about to make a run real quick. I'll be right back." I told Janaya as I grabbed my hoody from the closet.

"Where you going?" Janaya asked as she bit into her sandwich.

I hesitated. "Just to holla at a friend real quick. I'll be back."

My little sister smirked at me. "Yeah, whatever. Better strap-up."

I shook my head. "You outta pocket. It ain't even like that." I cracked up inside at what she said.

"Yeah, alright. I thought you said you was going to help me with my homework."

"Oh, I am. I ain't gon' be gone long."

Yani

"In and out, huh? Straight like that." She leaned over the counter laughing out loud while beating her fist against the top.

"Yo, chill!" I laughed. "I said it ain't like that. I'll be back. Get your other homework done and I'll help you with the other part when I get back. Don't leave the house and don't let nobody in here while I'm gone, either." I told her sternly.

"Yeah, yeah, yeah," she mumbled as she ate more of her sandwich.

I left out of the house and walked over to the 18 bus stop just as it was pulling up. I got on and rode over to Chew and Washington Lane before walking over to Tashai's house on Homer Street. It had started to get chilly out so I zipped up my jacket and threw the hood up over my head. A minute passed before Tashai answered the door after I rang the bell.

"Hey Davion," she said with a cute smile.

I smiled back. "What's up, Shorty?" She opened the door wider and let me in. Her mom had a nice house. It was a little smaller than ours. I looked around at the photos and paintings on the wall. They had a 40 inch flat-screen-TV in the living room with a PS4 connected to it. The tanned colored leather sofa had a throw blanket on it. Yeah, I knew what it was hitting for. I peeped that they also had a piano and for some reason I wondered who played.

"I can't get a hug?" she asked, snapping me out of my thoughts.

I grabbed her hand and pulled her over to me before wrapping my arms around her.

"What's good wit'chu?" I asked her as I let her go.

"Nothing. I was done my homework and was bored and thought about you and wanted you to come keep me company," she told me.

"Oh, you only think about me when you're bored?" I asked with a smirk.

"Naw, I'm not saying that," she said quickly and nervously.

"It's cool, Shorty. At least you thought about me."

I could tell that made her feel less tense when she smiled. I nodded at the piano.

"Who plays?" I asked her.

She turned and looked at the piano. "Oh, I do sometimes. My mom always wanted one when she

Yani

was younger and went out and bought it. She never plays it though, so I just started teaching myself how to play it. I ain't that good though."

"Yeah?" I asked with a raised brow beginning to get curious about her. "What do you know how to play?"

"Umm… I just learned how to play this old song by KC and Jo-Jo; *All My Life*," she told me as she walked over to the piano. The man in me couldn't help checking out her ass. She had a fat one, too.

Tashai sat at the piano and I stood next to her while she opened it up.

"I can't read music, this is just by ear so it might be a little off," she said. She sounded nervous and I noticed her hands were shaking a little. But when she started playing, you couldn't tell me this girl had never been officially taught. I watched her fingers move across the keys as she played the song hitting most of the rifts as she played. From what I could tell, she didn't make any mistakes.

"Yo that shit was dope," I told her when she was done.

"Thank you," she blushed. I began to feel bad that I automatically assumed she was hitting me up for a booty call. Maybe she really just wanted somebody to chill with her. I could dig it.

She played John Legend's *All of Me* and I found myself singing with her while she played. She then played One Republic's *Apologize* which was my favorite song when I was younger. It made me think of Joselyn.

"You got skills, Shorty. How come you didn't go to CAPA?" I asked her.

"I wanted to, but I had a C in Math and a C in Science so I didn't get in. Since they closed G-town high, King is my neighborhood school and I ended up there." Tashai told me as she closed the piano.

"Damn, I wouldn't send a dog there," I told her.

"I know, right? But it's not too bad. I mean, at least the work is easy. I practically got straight A's so getting into a good college should be cake."

"Yeah, you right." I replied. I noticed when she talked, she didn't use profanity which was a plus for her.

We talked for a little while about school, sports and everything in between. I peeped that she was heavy into topics dealing with racism, police brutality and was big on reading. She definitely was different from the other girls I had knocked off. She was funny as hell, too. I was starting to like her in a way that was different than most of the chicks I came across.

I looked up at her door and noticed it was dark out. I then looked at my phone.

"Oh shit, I gotta get back home. It's almost 7 o'clock. I was supposed to help my little sister with her homework."

"Oh, I'm sorry." Tashai apologized as we both stood up.

"It's cool, Shorty. You don't have to apologize. I was having so much fun bussing it up with you, I wasn't thinking about the time."

"Okay…" she trailed off. I detected a hint of sadness in her voice and for some reason, I thought back to when me and Janaya used to be left in the house by ourselves.

"Where your mom at, if you don't mind me asking?" I asked her when I got to the front door.

"She's at work. She works a lot. My dad isn't here anymore so she got a second job to make sure the house and everything is taken care of. It's a long story."

"Oh…" it was me that trailed off that time. "He left like moved out?"

"No… he was killed earlier this year." She lowered her eyes and I could tell the pain was still fresh.

"I'm sorry to hear that, Shorty. My mom died, too. Drug overdose when I was thirteen. Me and my sister found her dead in the house." I sighed and shook my head. "I don't want that depressing shit to kill our vibe, though. I had a good time with you. Can I call you later?"

That question made her blush and I smiled as I watched her try to hide it. She nodded her head. I gave her a hug. Even though she wasn't my girl, I wanted to kiss her, so I gave her a peck on the lips before leaving out.

"I'ma call you when I get in." I told her.

"Okay," she smiled again. "Good night Davion."

"Good night." I waited for her to close the door and then I made my way to the bus stop. My phone went off just as I was getting on the 18. It was Pops.

Yani

"Yo, Pops," I answered as I put my fare in the box and took a seat near the front. I saw one of the guys from Medary street and shook his hand.

"Where you at?" he asked me. He sounded angry.

"I went to go visit a friend. I just got on the 18. I should be home soon."

"You left your sister in the house by herself." Pops started.

"I know, Pops. I ain't expect to be gone this long. I'll be home in like 15 minutes."

"Yeah, alright." I disconnected the call and leaned back in my chair, thinking about Tashai all the way home.

Soon as I got in the door, Pops started ramming. "Ay, didn't I tell you before about leaving Jah-Jah in the house by herself?" Pops snapped. I took my hoody off and hung it up in the closet.

"My bad," I started.

"No, it's not *my bad*. You been doing this shit a lot now, lately. And I'm getting tired of repeating myself. When me and Meagan aren't home, unless y'all are going to Simon's for practice, on a school night, you're to stay your ass in the house."

"Since when?" I asked with a frown.

Pops looked at me as though I were crazy for questioning him. He never had a problem with us hanging out after school before so I didn't understand what the issue was now.

"You smelling yourself, questioning me. Bottom line, unless y'all are at Simon's or someplace I'm cool with y'all being at, I want y'all asses in the house. And you don't go no-where without checking with me first, understood?"

I shrugged my shoulders. "I guess."

"You was supposed to help your sister with her homework, but instead you out here laying dick with these lil' young thots."

I frowned at Pops. He was tripping. "Yo, it's not even like that, Dad. I ain't hitting none of these chicks off." I lied. I'd lost my virginity two years ago and was no stranger to getting my dick sucked, especially by those White girls at Central.

Pops looked at me sideways. "You might not have hit nothing tonight, but you far from a virgin. You just better be using those condoms I gave you. Because these little bitches see you making moves and they putting a bullseye on your wallet through your dick," Pops schooled me.

Yani

"Man, she ain't even like that." I slipped up. I cursed myself.

"Yeah, I knew it. And who is she?"

I shook my head as I grabbed a handful of grapes from off the dining room table and began popping them in mouth. "Her name is Tashai, Pops. She lives in Germantown and goes to King. But she ain't that type of girl, Pops. She plays the piano; she gets good grades. She's smart."

Pops looked at me for a moment. "Two red flags. She lives in Germantown and she goes to King."

I burst out laughing. "Come on, Pops. Seriously! You went to Dobbins and you're from G-Town."

"Yeah, but I'm a rare breed and that was back when all we dealt with were hoodlums and Muslims. Now-a-days, you got these pill popping niggas out here turned out as young as Jah-Jah age. All we had was weed, sex and alcohol," he replied as he shook his head. I snatched up some more grapes and put a couple in my mouth as Pops stared at me. "You like this girl?"

"Well, I went to middle school with her and just bumped into her Saturday when I was coming from the barber shop. We exchanged numbers and I hung out with her for a little bit." I fell silent for a moment as I thought about her. "Yeah, I like her. She's cool peoples."

Pops sighed. "Well, just remember what I said. You've got a lot going for yourself. Way more than I did when I was your age. Don't make the same mistakes I made. Strap up and don't let your dick get your ass in more trouble than you can handle."

I stared at Pops for a moment, thinking about the last thing he said. He always instilled in me to not make the same mistakes he made, but that was the first time that the way he said it made me feel like he was saying I was a mistake. Because after all, if he hadn't gotten Joselyn pregnant while they were in high-school, he wouldn't have been pressed to make money to make sure we were taken care of and probably never would have started selling drugs. He more than likely would have gone to college. But he could've taken the money he made selling drugs and used that to go to college. He chose to stay in the drug game. For greed, or for power, or for both, he chose.

Yani

"We all have choices…" I mumbled.

"You say something, son?" Pops asked from the kitchen.

"Nah. I'ma go help Janaya with her homework." I got up from the dining room table and walked upstairs. I tapped on Janaya's door.

"Yeah?" she replied.

"Can I come in?" I asked.

"Sure," Janaya replied blandly.

I opened her door and closed it behind me before sitting at her desk.

"I'm already done my homework. You were taking too long so I looked up how to do it on a Math site." Janaya said in a low voice as she drew in her sketchbook.

"My bad, Jah-Jah. I lost track of time. I ain't mean to leave you hanging like that."

"No, it's cool. Whatever."

"No, it's not cool. I should've helped you first before I left."

"Davion, I said it's cool. Like I said earlier, you're not always going to be around, so I gotta learn to look out for myself sometimes."

"Why do you keep saying that?" I asked my little sister.

"What?" she asked back, not looking up from her sketchbook.

"You keep saying I'm not going to always be around. I'm not going anywhere no time soon. At least I don't plan to," I told her.

"Yeah, I bet mom didn't plan to, either," she mumbled.

I fell silent not knowing what to say to that. It took me a moment to come up with something. "That was something way different. Something you were too young to understand then and are still too young understand now. As far as me, I'm your big brother. It's my job to look out for you even when you think you're too old for me to look out for you. We're going to be rolling around in wheel chairs when we're old as shit and I'ma still look out for you. Make sure they give you grape Kool-Aid because you hate cherry."

We both burst out laughing. "I told you, you's a weirdo, man." Janaya laughed.

I went over to her bed to see what she was drawing. My sister had mad skills. She was drawing a picture of Naruto throwing a punch at Sasuke as

Sasuke was dipping back to dodge it. Her detail and shadow work was on point.”

“That shit's lit,” I told her.

“Thanks, Dah-Dah,” she said with a smile.

I kissed her on the forehead. “Did you eat?”

“Yeah, Dad ordered some Chinese food. Yours is in the microwave.”

“Bet!” I said, hyped. I left her room and texted Tashai to let her know I was home and was about to eat dinner, but would call her as soon as I was done. She texted me *“Ok”* and I went downstairs to fuck up my food.

I sat on the phone with Tashai until well after 2AM knowing that we both had school in the morning. But the conversation between us was too much fun and I couldn't get enough of her voice. It was calming, but seductive at the same time. Up until talking to her, I had never been seduced before. Chicks were just down for whatever. Even though me and Tashai's conversations weren't sexual, she still aroused me. But it was more mentally than sexually, which was weird to me. It made me want to learn more about her.

“Hey, I think I just heard my mom come in. I better go to bed.” Tashai whispered into the phone.

"Alright, it's cool. I need to take my black ass to bed, anyway. I have practice in the morning and a game in the afternoon."

"Who do y'all play?" she asked in a whisper.

"Gratz. We 'bout to fuck that team up, too." I said arrogantly. Tashai giggled. "Why don't you come through and watch the game?"

She hesitated for a moment. "I'll try. Usually I go straight home from school. But I'll try. My mom is coming. I've gotta go." She quickly hung up the phone before I had a chance to say goodnight. I intertwined my fingers behind my head and looked up at the ceiling. I had stopped turning on the dino-lava lamp not long after Joselyn died. It reminded me too much of her. For some reason, I missed her at that moment and wished that she were around so she could meet Tashai. I was positive she would like her.

"I miss you, mom." I said with my eyes closed. Just as I was beginning to dose off, my phone vibrated with a text message. It was Tashai telling me goodnight.

"I was just thinking about you, Shorty. You about to have a boyfriend out here," I replied.

Yani

She sent a text back saying *"We'll see…"* with two heart-eyed emoji faces. I smirked. She was playing hard to get. But I could dig it though.

The next morning, Pops took me and Janaya to school as usual. I spent the whole day thinking about Tashai which was new to me. Not too many girls had held my attention this much for this long. I texted her good morning and was shocked she texted back. That afternoon, it was time to suit up. I heard that a few scouts from Georgetown, Mizzou and USC were going to be in the building. My top pick was USC. Even though I was only a junior, I was going to show the fuck out to make sure they came back the next year to check for me.

Lamar and I were still best friends and were at Central together. This was his first year on Varsity and he hadn't earned a starting position yet. Lamar had also shot up in height but was only 6'1. We dribbled the ball around practicing cross-overs and jump shots. Right before the end of practice which, was just before the players would be introduced so the game could start, Lamar threw me an oop and I banged that jawn in, setting off the crowd who had already gathered. Lamar and I ran at each other and jumped in the air, bumping one another with our shoulders. My coach blew the whistle so we could all come over to the bench.

"Alright Jones, I know you're excited, but calm down. You can show out when the game starts. Just remember, there's no *I* in team," my coach said as he looked us all over.

"Ain't no *we*, either." I joked as I tried to catch my breath. I was fired up. My teammates laughed.

"Watch it, now!" my coach mean-mugged me. He reminded us to play smart on the defensive end and not to ball hog on offense. "I know there are quite a few scouts here, but it's not about how many points you put on that board individually, but how well you play together collectively which will result in this win. Let's do this!"

I walked over to the bench and happened to look in the crowd. Janaya was just walking in. She waved at me and I waved back. She made her way over to the bleachers and took a seat. Just as I was getting in line so we could be introduced I saw Tashai sitting near the front of the bleachers. Her eyes were locked on me. She wiggled her fingers at me, saying hello and I waved back. It then dawned on me that I didn't see Pops or Meagan. Meagan was probably stuck at the shop and maybe Pops was running late. In all of my years playing ball, he never missed a game no matter what.

The players were introduced but when it came to me, the crowd went nuts. I had really established a name for myself over the last four years. I heard my sister's big mouth scream out, "That's my brother!" and laughed.

We dicked Gratz boots from the gate, starting off on a 22-0 run. We ended with a score of 88-67. I had 23 points, 7 assists, 12 rebounds, 5 offensive boards and 3 blocked shots. It was my best game of the season.

We got back to the locker room. It was a ritual for us to bang out a beat on the lockers while one of us danced. Kinda like a locker room Soul Train line, only better. I quickly showered and dressed and was on my way out when the coach stopped me.

"That was an amazing game, son. Amazing game."

"Thanks coach," I smiled.

"I was looking over your grades and noticed you're taking a couple of AP courses. I also noticed you have way more credits than the average junior. USC is really interested in you. They know you're a junior but are willing to bring you in on an early admission's ticket as well as give you a full scholarship if you pick up a few more classes so you can graduate early," the coach explained.

My eyes became wide. "You're kidding me, right?"

The coach shook his head. "Not at all. Here is a copy of the letter the recruiter left. You're going to receive another one in the mail."

Before the coach could finish what he was saying, I jumped up, throwing my fist in the air shouting, "Yes!"

"Talk it over with your parents. This is a big decision to make and shouldn't be made so hastily. They're giving you a week to decide only because it's the beginning of the second period and your counselor would have to move a lot of things in order to get you in those extra classes which will be three. Do you think you can handle that?" he asked me.

"Oh, I know I can," I said confidently. The coach smiled as he handed me the letter. I looked at it feeling so much pride. "Thanks so much, Coach. This is everything I've been working towards since 9th grade."

"I know, son. I know." The coach nodded his head with a smile. I left the office full of so much excitement. I couldn't wait to tell Janaya and Pops as well as Tashai and Meagan. When I got outside, only Tashai and Janaya were out there. I doubt they realized they were both waiting for me.

I looked around. "Jah-Jah, where's Pops and Meagan?"

Janaya shrugged her shoulders. "They weren't out here when I came out. They weren't outside of school to pick me up for the game so I hopped on the charter and caught the 26."

I frowned. That was weird. He never misses a game. I looked at Tashai and smiled. "What's up, Shorty?" She blushed when I gave her a hug. I saw the smirk on Janaya's face as she looked Tashai over as though she was sizing her up for approval. I shook my head. "Tashai, this is my little sister, Janaya. Janaya, this is Tashai."

"Hey," Janaya waved. Tashai smiled and waved back.

"Well, I don't know where Pops is but I'm hungrier than a mug. We usually get some pizza or something after one of our games but Pops ain't here so, y'all wanna go to Pizza Hut?" I asked as I looked from Tashai to Janaya.

"You know I'm with it," Janaya replied with a grin.

"Actually, I have to go home. My mom doesn't usually let me stay out on a school night," Tashai replied as she checked the time on her phone.

"We won't be out for long and I'll make sure you get back home okay," I told her as I threw my arm around her shoulder and pulled her close. It didn't take much persuasion before she gave in.

We walked over to Broad and Olney and caught the L bus to Stenton Ave and Washington Lane before heading into Pizza Hut. After ordering a large sausage and pepperoni pizza with bread sticks and honey chipotle wings with drinks, we sat over in a corner talking and laughing about the game. At first, Janaya wasn't saying much to Tashai, but after a few minutes, she warmed up to her, which made me feel better. I never brought a chick

Yani

around my family before, but since I liked Tashai, I wanted Janaya, Pops and Meagan to like her, too. I had texted Pops to let him know we won the game and to also talk to him about what the coach told me afterwards, but he didn't respond. In light of what happened with Joselyn, I began to worry.

"I'ma call a cab since it's kinda cold out. I'll be right back y'all." I went outside and called Pops first. He answered after the third ring.

"I can't talk right now, I'll call you later," he said quickly and then hung up. I looked at my phone with a frown.

"What the hell…?" I mumbled. I sent Pops a text message with three question marks and then called for a cab. They said they'd be there in five minutes. We packed up the rest of the food and went outside just as the cab pulled up. I had him take Tashai home first since she lived closest.

Tashai looked shocked when I opened the door for her and my sister to get in. When it was time to get out, I opened the door for her and grabbed her hand to help her out. I walked her to her front door.

"You played really good," Tashai told me when she got to the door.

"Thanks. My coach just told me if I take a couple more classes, I can graduate early and USC will give me an early admissions' ticket as well as a scholarship."

"Oh wow… that's amazing. You should go for it." Tashai encouraged me.

"Yeah, I gotta talk it over with my Pops first. But um… what's up with us?" I asked her.

Tashai blushed and shook her head. "Call me later."

"Yo, you really playing hard to get. It's cool. I'm patient." I leaned in to kiss her expecting her to back away but she didn't. She held my face while she kissed me.

"Not that hard," she whispered with a grin. I waited for her to go in the house and close the door before I went back to the cab.

"I'm telling Pops you out here kissing G-Town thots," Janaya said with a chuckle.

"Watch ya mouth, yo. She ain't no thot." I said seriously.

"It was just a joke… dag." Janaya said with a frown.

Yani

"Yeah well, don't play like that again." I warned her. I could tell I upset Janaya a little so I sighed and elbowed her. "I just better not catch you out here kissing no North Filthy niggas." Janaya smiled and elbowed me back.

"Whatever. You talk to Pops?" she asked me.

"I called him but he was real short with me. I don't know what was up with that. He said he'd call back though," I told her.

"I wonder why he wasn't at the game," Janaya mused.

"Yeah… me too." We got to the house and the fair was a little over $20. I gave the cabby a dub and a five and told him to keep the change.

When I turned the key and opened the door, I thought I was going to have a heart attack. The house was a fucking wreck. Sofa cushions were thrown about. Stuff from book cases were all over the floor. I didn't know if we had been robbed or what.

"Oh my God!" Janaya shrieked.

"Stay right here," I told my little sister. I dropped my duffle bag and pushed the door open hard to make sure nobody was behind it. I didn't know what the fuck happened or what I should expect when I went in the house. My heart was in my fucking throat as I went inside. The first place I went was to the safe that Pops had in the wall. After I saw him go in it when he paid for Joselyn's funeral, I waited until I was home alone to try every combination of numbers I thought meant something to him before I finally got it open. He always kept a shit load of money in there as well as a 9MM. I hurriedly opened the safe, took the gun out and closed it.

"Dah-Dah!" Janaya called me sounding like she was crying.

"Stay outside, Janaya. I mean it!" I shouted to her. I took the safety off the gun and aimed it at the kitchen before peeking in. I then opened the basement door and turned the light on, aiming down the stairs. I didn't see anybody but something deep inside of me told me not to go down there.

Instead, I decided to go upstairs and check the bedrooms. All of our rooms were tossed just like downstairs except whoever had been in our home had more mercy on me and Janaya's room than Pops' and Meagan's room. What the fuck was going on?

Yani

I checked all of the rooms, under the beds, in the closets and the bathroom. Nobody was in there. I was about to let out a sigh of relief when Janaya started screaming.

"Davion! Davion somebody just came out the basement and went out the back door!!" Janaya screamed.

I bolted down the stairs and ran out the front. Grabbing Janaya's hand, I pulled her with me as we hauled ass down the street to a neighbor's house.

"Mr. Alexander!" I yelled as I knocked on his door rapidly. "Mr. Alexander, it's Davion!"

"Just a minute, wait a second. I'm coming!" he yelled back to us as he hurried to the door.

"What in blue-blazes is the problem?" he asked as he looked at us wildly when he opened the door.

"Somebody was in our house when we just came home. I don't know if they were trying to rob us, but, Janaya saw them come out the basement while I was checking upstairs." I said to him quickly as I tried to catch my breath.

I noticed Mr. Alexander wasn't looking at me, he was looking at the gun in my hand.

"Where did you get that gun, son?" he asked me calmly.

I looked down at it, forgetting that I had it in my hand. Janaya looked at me with wide eyes. I could tell she was terrified. "It's my father's. When I saw the house was tossed after I opened the door, I took it from the safe and was just looking through the house with it," I explained.

Mr. Alexander swallowed. "Give me the gun, son. We'll call the police and your father. But if the cops see you with that gun, you're going down for at least five years. Give it to me and I'll give it to your father when he comes."

"But he doesn't know I know the combination to his safe. He might snap out. I can put it back without him knowing," I said in return, now becoming frightened.

"What do you think would upset him more? His son going to jail for possession of a weapon or knowing you can crack a safe? Give me the gun and we'll call the cops from your cell phone so the cops don't show up here, but your house instead."

I handed over the gun to Mr. Alexander and then called the cops, telling them everything that

Yani

happened, but left out the part about me taking the gun from my father's safe. Twenty minutes later, they were pulling up the street. I jogged up to the house to meet up with them with Janaya following behind me.

"Are you the owner of this house?" the first officer asked me.

"No sir, I'm the owner's son…" I began explaining to the cop what I knew as far as coming home and seeing that our house had been tossed. I then told him that Janaya saw someone come out of the basement and run out the back of the house.

"Did she get a good look at him?" he asked as his radio went off. He stepped over some books that had been thrown on the floor in the dining room and went over to the basement door.

"All I saw was that he had on all black and had a hood over his head. If I had to guess how tall he was, I would say maybe a little taller than me. Like maybe 5'9 or something. It happened so fast…" Janaya explained as she followed behind us.

A few more cops came into the house and began looking upstairs as the officer we were with shined a light down into the basement. After thoroughly checking down there, he came back up and took out a small notepad from his jacket pocket.

"Where are your parents?" the officer asked me.

"My father owns a supermarket and my step-mom owns a hair salon in Mount Airy. I'm guessing they're both still at work since they weren't at my basketball game." I told him.

"And your mother?" he asked as he peered up at me.

"She's dead, sir." I said as I looked at the floor.

"I'm sorry to hear that." He jotted down a few things and then got the name and addresses to Pops' supermarket as well as Meagan's hair salon. A unit was sent over to the supermarket but Pops wasn't there. Another unit was sent to Meagan's salon. Janaya and I rode with them. I watched from the back of the squad car as the officer talked to Meagan. I was expecting her to have a look of fear and worry on her face. Instead, she looked more nervous. I would go as far as to say even a tad guilty. What the hell was going on?

Yani

I got out of the squad car and Janaya was about to follow me as always. "Stay here," I said to her sternly.

I walked over to the officer and Meagan. Everything the officer was asking her, she shook her head and answered, "I don't know." Either Pops trained her well or she really had no clue as to what the fuck he was into.

"Have you heard from my dad?" I asked Meagan once the cop stopped firing questions her way.

"Not since this morning. My God, I'm so glad you and Jah-Jah are okay! I can't believe someone would want to break into our house. We've lived there for almost twelve years and never had any problems. Was anything stolen?" Meagan asked.

I peered at her. "I didn't get a chance to check and see. We were tripping over the fact that somebody broke in." I replied.

Meagan stood with her hand clutching her chest as she shook her head. She then grabbed her phone and called Pops. It went straight to voicemail. "Cortez, you need to call me immediately. It's an emergency. Better yet, wherever you are, whatever you're doing, drop it and get over to the salon, now!" she said into the phone before hanging up quickly.

The cop advised Meagan to go through the home to make sure nothing was stolen and also told her that if anything was missing, to come over to the police station to file a police report immediately. She thanked the officer and shook his hand before he left with his partner.

Something was nagging at me about what was going on. Meagan was acting funny and I was starting to get the feeling that she knew more about that break-in than she was letting on.

She was able to get one of her associates to handle locking up the salon when the last client was finished and we hopped in her Honda CRV. She sped back to the house and went inside without a lick of fear. Meagan looked around and I was beginning to see how furious she was. She shook her head as she began placing the sofa cushions back on the chair.

"Thank God we weren't here," she mumbled. "He more than likely would have killed us."

Janaya didn't hear her, but I damned sure did. "What'd you say?" I asked her.

Yani

She jumped as though I startled her. "Nothing, I was just thinking out loud."

"You said *he*… do you know who did this?" I asked her.

"No…" she hesitated. "I was talking about the guy Jah-Jah said she saw run out the back door while you were checking upstairs. You shouldn't have came in here. Once you saw the house was tossed like this, you should've ran to a neighbor's house and dialed 9-1-1. Your dad would never forgive himself if something happened to either of you," she scolded me as she continued to pick up pillows and over turned dining room chairs. She kicked one out of frustration. "I'm not doing this shit tonight," she sneered before storming into the kitchen.

Something was off with Meagan. I didn't believe for one second she was talking about the guy Jah-Jah saw leaving out the back of the house. I looked over at my little sister who had sat on the couch and looked like she was nodding off.

"Go to bed, Janaya." I told her.

"I wanted to wait for Pops to get home," she whined.

"You can see him in the morning. It's late. Go to bed."

She sucked her teeth as she got up from the couch and sulked up the stairs. I went up behind her and helped her fix her bed good enough so she could get in it and go to sleep. I felt like Meagan at that moment. I wasn't cleaning up shit.

I went to my room and cleared a path to my bed before fixing it. My phone had died during the whole ordeal after the cops had gotten to the house. I plugged it in and turned it on only to see that I had a few text messages from Tashai.

"Yo Shorty. It was some drama at the house so I couldn't call you. I'ma holla at you in the morning before I go to school, alright?" I texted her back.

"Are you okay?" she asked in return.

"Not really. But I'ma talk to you about it in the morning. Thanks again for coming to my game. Good night." She texted me back to say good night and then I laid across my bed intending to wait up for Pops, but fell asleep.

The sound of Pops' angry voice jerked me awake from my sleep. I wiped the corner of my mouth and strained to listen. It sounded like him

Yani

and Meagan were arguing. I came out of my room and crept down a few of the steps so I could hear better.

"You told me when we got this house that the hustling shit was going to stop. But then you wanted to fight for the kids and had to get a lawyer and wanted to make sure that the lawyer fees didn't eat through our savings, so you insisted that you needed to grind a little longer. Then the kids came and you claimed you needed to adjust to being a full-time father and you insisted you made sure we had enough money. I was fine with that. Now this shit with Constantine is getting out of hand. I'm getting threats at the shop! They're running up in our house! You're disappearing and not telling me anything! What the hell is going on, Cortez!?"

I continued to ear hustle as my heart thudded in my chest. Meagan was being threatened? Was my father in trouble?

"I said I have everything under control, babe. I know what I'm doing. I'm not going to let these niggas think they can just push over me. This is my shit that I built from nothing and I'm not just going to let that muthafucka strong arm me and take what's mine. Fuck that," my father seethed.

"Oh my God, Cortez! There is so much more at stake than your pride. What if I had been home? Or worse, what if the kids had been here?" Meagan said close to tears. "We have enough money. Why can't you bow out and retire?!"

"Meagan, I said I've got this. I have a meeting set up with these cats on Friday. Everything will be squared away. Business will be handled and we'll be good, alright? Trust me," Pops said to her as he rubbed her neck before kissing her. I figured he would be heading upstairs, so I crept back to my room and got back into bed. A moment later, Pops was coming in my room.

"Davion, get up," he said to me.

I sat up in the bed and he clicked the light on before closing the door behind himself. He looked at me for a moment. "How long have you known about the safe in the wall?" he asked me.

I swallowed past a lump of fear in my throat. "Since you paid for Joselyn's funeral." I said back to him with a straight face. He stared at me for a moment. Usually he would check me over referring to my mother as Joselyn. Tonight, for whatever reason, he let it slide.

Yani

"I understand your need to be a hero tonight. I commend you for that. But a smart man knows when to run. It doesn't make him a coward," my father said to me.

I stared at him for a moment as I made sure I chose my words carefully. "A smart man knows when to retire too, right? That wouldn't make him a coward."

"As I said; a smart man knows when to run. This isn't something I wanted you to ever be a part of which is why I tried my damndest not to ever let the bullshit touch my front door. Unfortunately, today, it has. So, lessons need to be learned. I'll leave it at that." Pops sighed deeply as though he was extremely tired. "I heard you had a good game today."

"Yeah, I did," I replied with a grin. I then gave Pops the rundown of what happened when we played Gratz, saving the best part for last. I reached inside of my book bag and showed him the letter.

"Coach told me that USC is really interested in me. They're going to give me a full scholarship as well as an early admissions' ticket as long as I take on a few more classes so I can graduate a year early."

The look of pride Pops held after hearing what I said was something I'll never forget. He gave me a firm handshake and then hugged me before slapping me on the back.

"I'm proud of you, son. This is a big decision for you to make."

"I know. And I really want to do it. I know I can do it. I just wanted to run it by you first to see what you thought." I explained.

"If you feel deep down inside that this is a great opportunity for you, and I feel like it is also, then you have my approval. Go for it. I'm behind you one thousand percent."

"That means a lot, Pops. It really does." I said as I looked at the letter again with a huge grin.

"Get some sleep and we'll talk about it some more tomorrow. But for now, other than basketball practice, I want you and Jah-Jah to come straight home from school. I know you have a little girlfriend now, but until I vet her, you're gonna have to chill for a bit."

"Seriously, Pops?" I asked before shaking my head.

Yani

"I'm not playing, boy. When things calm down, we can negotiate and maybe she can come over for dinner. Until then, I want y'all asses in this house." I leaned back on my pillow and shook my head. I couldn't believe how strict he was being with us because of the stupid shit he had gotten into.

"You're already becoming a better man than I was at your age. Stay focused and you'll become a better man than I could've ever hoped to be. I'm damned proud of you, son. And I know your mother is proud of you, too." And with those words, Pops cut out my light and closed my bedroom door.

The one thing that remained constant with my father was making sure that I turned out better than he did. I don't think I understood how much it took for him to be able to say the words he said to me that night.

The rest of the week dragged on. Even though I should have been excited because of my pending decision with USC, I was distracted by what happened with the break in and whatever issues Pops was having with his "business". As much as I wanted to, I couldn't see Tashai after school. The weekend was even worse, but Jah-Jah and I made the best of it by playing video games. Since school was closed Monday, I couldn't wait to get there Tuesday so I could speak with the counselor and have the extra classes added to my roster so I could move forward with USC.

I hauled-ass down the hall to the counselor's office, whose name was Mr. Floyd, only to see that his door was closed, locked and his light was out. I checked the time on my cell-phone and saw that it was 7:45AM. I knew for sure that the coach was in. I ran over to his office and knocked on his door.

"Come in," he called out. I walked inside and saw that he was going through his file cabinet. "Take your hat off, Davion," he said without looking at me.

I snatched my hat off quickly and cleared my throat. "Coach Thompson, do you know what time the counselor is going to be in?" I asked.

"He's going to be out of the building for the week. I believe he is coming back Friday sometime in the afternoon." The coach turned and looked at me. "I take it you already made a decision."

Yani

"Yeah. I'm gonna go. I talked to my Pops and my step-mom and they both said they would support my decision one thousand percent," I sighed feeling a little disappointed. "It sucks that the counselor won't be back until Friday."

"Well, that will give you enough time to think over this and change your mind if you want to."

"I doubt that I will, though." I mumbled. The coach studied my face for a moment before sitting on the edge of his desk.

"Everything alright, son?" he asked me.

I shook my head. "I'm just thinking about the moment I was positive that I wanted to play basketball and everything that's happened since then. I kinda don't want to leave my sister. But at the same time, I want to show her that despite what we've been through, dreams can come true."

The coach smiled, "Your sister will be here next year, right?"

"She has an interview here Wednesday. I think this is her top pick, so yeah."

"Good. I look forward to helping with coaching her. We're definitely going to miss you," the coach told me. He stood up and gave me a pat on the back just as the first bell was ringing.

"See you at practice today," I said to the coach before leaving his office. Words couldn't describe how excited I was to be taking this next step towards realizing my dream. But for a brief moment, I began to second guess my decision. I worried about Janaya and who would look after her while I was gone. I shook my head as I walked to my locker and silently told myself that was just my mind trying to look for a way out because of fear of failure. With this though, failure was not an option.

I quickly texted Tashai to tell her good morning and then got down to business for school.

After practice, later that afternoon I checked my phone to see that Janaya texted me to let me know that she didn't feel comfortable going home without me being there so she went to the library on Ogontz avenue. I let her know I would be there soon. I also saw I had a couple text messages from Tashai wanting to know if I could come over to keep her company.

"My bad, Shorty. I just got outta practice. I gotta take care of some things at home with my Pops so I can't come today. But maybe we can hang out after school tomorrow." I

Yani

sent the text as I walked towards Broad and Olney so I could catch the 6 bus and pick Janaya up from the library.

My phone rang and I saw that it was Meagan. It's rare that she calls my phone. I answered to see what she wanted.

"Yo, Meagan what's up?" I asked as I jogged across the street before the light turned red.

"Have you heard from your dad?" she asked me.

"Naw. I just got out of practice. Why, what's up?"

"A couple of the ladies that work at the store hit me up, wondering where he was. He was supposed to sign off on some supplies but his manager had to do it in his place this morning. Christa says he still hasn't shown up," Meagan explained in a quiet voice.

"Did you call his phone?" I asked. I took out my school transpass and boarded the bus before making my way to the back.

"I've been calling his phone and texting him all day but he isn't answering or replying."

I sucked my teeth. "He did this crap last week. It's starting to get on my nerves, man. Ain't nobody got time for this." I said with an attitude. "I'll see if I can get him on the phone and then I'll call you back." I told Meagan.

"Okay," she said before hanging up.

The bus pulled from the depot with the glare from the sun setting hitting my eyes. I squinted as I scrolled through my contacts before getting to Pops' number and dialing it. I thought about the week before and how our house had been tossed. A name had been mentioned along with some other shit. Threats made to Meagan at the shop, street beef my Pops had with a nigga named Constantine. Unanswered calls. What the hell was going on?

Pops' phone rang twice and then it sounded like someone picked up.

"Hello?" I spoke into the phone. Some dickhead on the bus was playing phone DJ, blasting the shit out of a Drake song. I cut my eyes at him before placing a finger in my ear so I could hear better. "Pops, can you hear me? Hello…?"

The phone cut off. I looked at my screen and then dialed him again. This time, it was as if someone answered but then hung right up. I called right back and the same thing happened. I got a bad feeling. I was going to wait a moment and then call back but decided not to wait. This time the phone went straight to voicemail.

"Ay Pops, what's up with your phone? Call me when you get this. Meagan and Christa's been trying to get a hold of you all day. Can you call one of us to let us know what's up? Peace, Pops." I hesitated a moment before disconnecting the call. I then called Meagan back.

"I didn't get him on the phone. Maybe he's in a meeting or something," I suggested.

"No, he didn't have any meetings today. He was only supposed to go into the store and do paperwork and deliveries. That's what he does every Tuesday."

I became quiet again. Meagan knew his schedule better than I did. I didn't know what to think at the moment. But I definitely had a bad feeling. "I'll try to get him on the phone again after I pick Janaya up from the library," I told her.

"Okay. Call me as soon as you talk to him. Better yet, tell him I said to bring his ass to the salon."

"Alright." I disconnected the call and tapped my finger on the screen. Something was going on with Pops and shit was about to get real, real quick.

I got to the library and was surprised to see Lamar sitting with Janaya while she had her books opened. It looked like he was helping her with her homework. But if I didn't know any better, I was positive Janaya was blushing. I mean, she was seriously geeking next to him. Let me put the brakes on this shit right now.

"What's up, Mar?" I spoke as I walked over to them. Janaya looked up at me startled and appearing nervous. I pretended not to notice. Lamar on the other hand, looked cool as beans. I slapped him a handshake. "Why you ain't come to practice?"

"I had a job interview at the Rite-Aid around the corner on Ogontz Ave. Then I popped in here to look for that book Ms. Cohens wants us to use for class and saw Janaya. I was just helping her with her math homework real quick," Lamar explained.

"Thanks, homie. I appreciate that. Did you get the gig?" I asked.

Yani

"Yeah, I come back to do my paper work tomorrow and then I start next Monday." Lamar told me as he gathered up his stuff. I nodded my head and then looked at Janaya. She had her face in her book looking as though she was hard at work. She's normally never this quiet. Something was definitely up.

Lamar slapped me another handshake. "Alright, hit me up later my G so I can bust your ass in some NBA 2k14."

"Never nigga. But I got you," I laughed. I waited until Lamar was out of ear shot before I looked down at Janaya. "Don't even think about it, Jah-Jah."

"What'chu talking 'bout, Dah-Dah?" Janaya asked innocently as she packed up her book bag.

"Yo, I saw the way you were geeking over here with Lamar. That nigga's 16 and you're only 13."

Janaya frowned at me and cut me off. "First off, I don't geek over no nigga. Second of all, this over protecting big brother role is getting mad old. And third, stop blocking." She laughed at her last comment before putting her jacket on.

"Man, whatever. I saw you blushing and everything so don't try to play. You ain't even low with yours."

Janaya waved me off and we walked out of the library. I looked in my phone and saw that I had a text from Tashai but still nothing from Pops. Instead of responding to her, I tried calling him again. It went straight to voicemail. I huffed and shook my head as I stuffed my phone back in my pocket.

"What's wrong?" Janaya asked me as we hopped on the XH to ride to the Cheltenham Depot.

"Meagan ain't heard from Pops all day and been trying to get a hold of him but couldn't. I'm calling this nigga, too, but he ain't answering his phone."

"Again?" Janaya asked me as we sat down. "What's up with him? He's been acting real strange lately."

I hesitated before responding to my sister. As far as I knew, she didn't know anything about Pops being a major distributer in the drug business. "I

Yani

don't know," I mumbled instead. "Have you heard from him?" I asked.

Janaya shook her head. We both fell silent as we rode to the bus depot. As soon as we got off, the H bus pulled up. We jumped on it and headed home.

In light of what happened the week before, I was nervous as hell about going in the house. Tentatively, I put my key in and unlocked the door. I saw where Meagan finally finished cleaning everything up but still wasn't too sure about going in. Up until today, Meagan or Pops made sure they were home when we got in. When Pops got home, I was going to make sure I run it by him that it might not be a bad idea to get an alarm system.

Janaya and I walked through the house, making sure everything was kosher. After we were satisfied that it was, I called Meagan.

"Did you get him on the phone?" Meagan asked as soon as she answered, skipping past hello.

"No. I was just about to ask if you had heard from him yet." I sighed. "When I called, it sounded like he answered but he didn't say anything and then we were cut off. I called back and he picked up and hung right back up. The couple times I called back after that, it went straight to voicemail."

I peeped over my shoulder to see where Janaya was. No surprise she was in the kitchen grabbing a snack. I lowered my voice. "Yo Meagan, what's really going on? I heard you and Pops talking the other night. Is he in some kind of trouble?"

Meagan hesitated and the phone conversation was suddenly filled with dead air. Finally, she cleared her throat. "It's nothing he can't handle and it's not anything you should be worried about. I'm on my way home. If he gets in before me, let him know to call me, okay?" she asked me.

"All right," I said to her before disconnecting the call. I could feel it in the air that something wasn't right. I wasn't sure what it was, but I hoped Pops was good. We had already lost Joselyn. I couldn't imagine what life would be like if we lost Pops, too.

"Is Dad on his way home?" Janaya asked from the kitchen.

"I think he's at a meeting," I lied. Fact of the matter was; I didn't know where the hell he was. My phone rang. Without looking at it, I answered.

"Pops?" I said into the phone.

Yani

"It's Tashai... hey."

"Oh, my bad, Shorty. What's up?" I spoke back. I grabbed my duffle bag from off of the floor and made my way up to my room. I saw where Meagan had cleaned everything up in there, too. Good looking.

"Nothing. Just in the house by myself again and wanted someone to talk to," she told me.

As alluring as her voice was, I wasn't focused on Tashai at the moment. My mind was on my dad, worried as to whether or not he was good. She was talking, and I barely caught a word she said.

"Did you hear me?" I heard her ask.

"Huh? My fault. What did you say?"

"If you're busy, I can call you back."

I hesitated for a moment as I had an idea. "Actually, I'm about to take care of some stuff around the house. I'ma hit you back later, all right?" Before I gave her a chance to respond, I disconnected the call.

I crept down the hall to Pops' and Meagan's room and went inside. I started looking around, not having any idea what I was even fucking looking for.

Hoop Dreams Deflated

I checked in the usual spots that people liked to hide things; under the bed, under the mattress, in dresser drawers, and then finally, the top of the closet. There was nothing in those places that could give me an idea as to what was going on with Pops and who the hell Constantine was. I plopped down on Pops' and Meagan's bed trying to think. Completely at a loss without any clue as to what I should do or where I should look next, I got up so I could leave their room. Just as I was about to fix the bed back from where I checked under the mattress, I saw it. The thick, heavy, cherry wood headboard looked a little off. I then thought of the painting on the wall downstairs and how it was not an ordinary painting, but really a safe, something that could easily be over looked, and wondered if that was the case with the headboard. I felt around the bottom of it, pressing lightly with my fingertips. I didn't get any results while feeling around the side but when I touched the top, I heard a *click* sound and froze. The face of the headboard shifted and I was able to slide it downward.

Pops had some crazy hiding spots. But what was even crazier was what was hidden in the headboard. There was an external drive, a wad of cash and what looked like SD cards taped to the back of the headboard, all of them labeled with some kind of code that made no sense to me.

"What the fuck…?" I mumbled to myself.

"Davion!" I heard Meagan call out to me.

"Oh shit!" I murmured. I tried to slide the headboard face back into place but couldn't get it to stay. I fumbled around with it as my heart thudded in my chest, hoping I got it secured before Meagan came upstairs.

"Come on, come on, come on!" I panicked. I finally heard the *click* sound again. My hands trembled as I slowly pulled them away, praying that the face of the headboard stayed. When it didn't move, I jumped from the bed and quickly fixed the sheets just as I heard Meagan approaching the room.

"What are you doing in here?" she asked me with a look of suspicion.

"Dad had my Malcolm X book and I was getting it for a writing assignment I have." I lied.

She continued to look at me suspiciously before her face softened up. She then went over to the bigger dresser and retrieved the book for me. "Here you go," she said as she handed it to me.

I took it from her and asked, "You heard from Pops?"

Meagan sighed before shaking her head. "No." She then looked at her watch. "Maybe he did have a meeting that I forgot about. It's so much shit going on, sometimes it's hard to keep up."

I stared at her for a moment waiting for her to elaborate. For whatever reason, she couldn't look at me.

"I guess I'll go get my homework started," I mumbled before leaving the room.

Homework was the last thing on my mind once I was in my bedroom with the door closed. What the hell was on those SD cards and that hard drive that Pops felt like he had to hide them in his head board? I decided the minute Meagan left the house for whatever reason, I was going to get one of the cards to see what was on them.

My phone vibrated and I saw that I had a text message from Tashai.

"I'ma holla at you later, Shorty. I'm about to knock out this homework and then clean my room." I tossed my

phone on the bed and then laid across it. Still no word from Pops. Where was he? Not meaning to, I fell asleep.

My room was pitch black when I woke up and I had no idea what time it was. I looked at my phone and saw that it was after midnight. Damn, I slept through dinner and no one came to get me. My mind skipped past dinner and went straight back to Pops. I got up from my bed and left my room, heading straight to his. Only a lamp was lit, but he wasn't in there and neither was Meagan. Out of habit, I peeked my head inside of Janaya's room. She was snuggled up under her blankets, sound asleep. After silently closing her door, I went over to the stairs. I could hear Usher's song *Moving Mountains* playing softly and wondered if Pops and Meagan were downstairs cuddled up on the couch. I went downstairs to say what's up to Pops but didn't see him. Meagan was instead sitting at the counter with a glass of red wine next to her. Her hands were folded together and she was leaning on them. If I didn't know any better, it sounded like she was crying.

"Meagan?" I called to her causing her to jump. She quickly tried to wipe her eyes and then turned her back to me, pretending to be looking for something. "Where's Pops?"

"He didn't get in yet." she replied.

"Wait, he hasn't been at home at all? Did he call or text or anything?" I asked. Now I was really worried. Meagan shook her head with her back to me. Naw, fuck this.

I walked over to her and turned her around so she could face me. Her eyes were red as though she had been crying for a while. "What's going on, Meagan? Like seriously, what's up? Pops don't never go a whole day without calling or texting and he always answers his phone or at the very least, hits us right back if he misses our calls. What's good, yo?"

"I don't know," Meagan said as her eyes teared up. "In all my years of being with him, I never had to worry about him coming home. He always came home no matter what." She put her hand to her mouth and broke down in tears. I started to hug her but then changed my mind.

"Did you call the cops?" I asked instead.

Yani

She nodded her head as she sniffed. "They said he had to be missing for at least twenty-four hours before they could do anything."

"Fuck that!" I hissed, not even caring about cursing in front of her. "Anything can happen to him in twenty-four hours. Something could've already happened, like what the fuck!?"

"Davion! I know you're upset. I'm just as pissed and scared as you. But you need to watch your mouth." Meagan said to me sternly.

I took a deep breath, trying to calm down. "What about Buck and Sam. Did you holla at them? Have they heard from him?" I asked. They were my dad's closest friends who were like uncles to me. If anybody knew anything, I was sure they did.

"They were the first ones I hit up. They haven't heard from him either but said they would put their ears to the streets to see what's up," she said in return. She shook her head again and took a deep breath. "I just want him to come home. I can't go to sleep without him. Not until I know he's okay."

I felt bad at that moment, suspecting that Meagan knew more than what she led on to. She really did love my father.

Hoop Dreams Deflated

I reached in the downstairs closet and grabbed a blanket and a pillow, insisting that she lay down at least for a little while. She declined at first but then decided to do as I suggested. Pulling her shoes off and putting the blanket over her before kissing her on the forehead took me back to the day I did that for Joselyn when she came home high after stealing Janaya's money. It left me with a sad, sickening feeling, as I then longed for my mother.

I went upstairs and laid across my bed before grabbing my phone. I then opened my Instagram Page and posted a recent picture of Pops:

"This is my dad, Cortez. We haven't seen him or heard from him since this morning. We've been calling and texting him all day and he isn't responding back or answering his phone and this ain't like him at all. He always comes home and he always answers his phone no matter what. His wife means the world to him, and me and my sister even more. He always comes home! If anybody hears from him or knows where he is, hit me or his wife Meagan up. Please share this and help bring my Pops home." I posted the phone number and made sure I put the same post on Facebook as well. Then I said a small prayer to

myself. "Please God, you already got my mom. Don't take my dad, too. Please."

My phone vibrated with notifications of people who liked the post, shared it and commented to let me know we were in their prayers and they would do their best to keep an eye out for him. I had a sinking feeling that this shit was going to end badly.

My alarm blasted Meek Mill, snatching me out of my sleep. I literally felt like I had just closed my eyes. After finding my bearings, I immediately grabbed my phone and checked my notifications on Instagram and Facebook. I had over forty-two shares which comforted me a bit. It at least let me know that there would be more eyes out looking for him. I saw that I had a comment from Lamar.

"My mom said she saw him sitting in his car over near Limekiln Pike yesterday right before 1 o'clock. I'll check to see if his car is around there on my way to school."

I didn't even think to look for his car! I sent a reply back to Lamar. *"Thanks, my nig! Let me know!"* I scrolled through some of the other comments quickly, most of which were useless, and then got up to take my shower and get ready for school.

Janaya burst in my room as I was getting dressed. Thank God I already had my drawls on!

"Ay yo! What the hell, Jah-Jah? Knock nigga, shit, you coulda caught me butt-ass naked in here!" I scolded her.

"Screw that! Where is Daddy? What is this mess I'm getting on Facebook, people writing on my wall asking if we're good and this post of yours all up and down my news feed talking about he's missing?" She sounded like she was damn near about to have a heart-attack.

"Chill out, man. I'm just trying to get some extra eyes out there to keep a look out for him, that's all," I said nonchalantly.

Janaya shook her head. She wasn't trying to hear that shit. "No! If Daddy didn't come home last night, we need to call the police. What the hell is Facebook going to do?"

"Watch your mouth, yo. And Meagan already called the police. They said he had to be missing for at least twenty-four hours before they could do anything. Besides, Lamar just said that Ms. Aretha saw him sitting in his car near Limekiln Pike

Yani

yesterday around one. He's going to see if his car is still around there and then let me know."

"Why wouldn't he come home, though?" Janaya asked. She bit her lip, trying to hold back her tears.

I sighed not knowing what to tell her. "Get dressed so you can be ready for your interview with Central. Pops will be alright."

Janaya turned to leave my room and then stopped. "Yeah… I thought mom was going to be alright, too." She left my room before I could respond. A knot of fear tightened up in my stomach as I thought over what she said. I finished getting dressed and then went downstairs. Meagan was asleep on the couch. I tapped her lightly and she jumped up.

"Cortez?" she mumbled as she looked around.

I shook my head. "No, Meagan. It's me. Lamar said Ms. Aretha saw him sitting in his car yesterday on Limekiln Pike around one and he's going to walk around there before school to see if his car is still on the block and let me know."

Meagan nodded her head and then put her hands to her face. I couldn't bare knowing the pain she was in over not knowing where he was. I then thought of something.

"I left my book upstairs, I'll be back." I jetted back upstairs and went into their room. The face of the head board slid down with ease this time and I quickly swiped one of the SD cards, intending to put it in my MacBook so I could see what was on it. I left out the room and went back downstairs.

"Let me get up so I can take you two to school," Meagan said as she strained to sit up.

"No, you don't have to. Jah-Jah has an interview at Central today. Stay here just in case Pops comes back." I said to her. Meagan hesitated for a minute and then nodded her head in agreement.

My phone went off. I thought it was a message from Tashai telling me good morning. Instead it was something on Facebook Messenger. I didn't know who the person was and started not to open it, but then thought that maybe it was somebody who had info on Pops.

"You'll find that nigga where you fucking smell him!" the message read. I froze in mid-step as my heart thudded in my chest. I clicked on the person's

profile to see who the hell they were, but it looked like a dummy profile with a pic of a Rottweiler as the profile image. The profile literally had been created that morning.

"Who the fuck is this?" I typed back. *"Yo, don't fucking play on some nut-ass shit like this, pussy. Who the fuck are you?"* I was heated inside, unsure if this person was serious or was just starting shit. Niggas do be on some ignorant shit even when something serious like this is going on.

"You ain't built like that Dah-Dah. Neither was your fucking "Pops"."

This was definitely somebody who knew us. I then calmed down and dismissed it as somebody who I probably fucked up previously for disrespecting Joselyn.

"What's wrong?" Janaya asked me as she came from the kitchen with a baggy filled with grapes.

I shook my head and adjusted my duffle bag on my shoulders. "Nothing."

We got to Central just as Lamar was crossing the street from getting off the 26 going in the opposite direction. We slapped each other a handshake.

"What's up, yo? Did you see it?" I asked immediately.

Lamar shook his head. "Naw. He drives a 2014 black Impala, right?"

I nodded my head. "Yeah."

"Naw, it wasn't around there. But one of the old heads said he was talking to some 'bol, and then got in his car and followed him somewhere."

"When was this?" I asked.

"I guess not long after my mom saw him. She said he looked like he was having a heated convo with somebody so she just waved, got her eggs and milk from the Papi store, and came back home."

I thought back to the message that was sent to me that morning.

"Hey Mar," Janaya spoke with a smile.

"What's up?" Lamar spoke back nonchalantly. Yeah, he knew better. I saw Janaya's face crack at the way he did the Matrix pass her vague attempt to flirt with him. Yeah, I knew she was crushing on him.

"Let me walk Janaya to the office and then I'll see you in advisory." I said to Lamar. He nodded and went on his way.

Yani

"You ain't even low with yours," I said to Janaya as I shook my head.

"What are you talking about, now?" she asked back.

I shook my head. "Yeah, whatever. Don't make me hurt you, yo. Seriously. He's too old for you."

"All I said was hi," she said with a smile.

"Yeah, don't get home-boy fucked up out here." I warned her.

"Oh my God!" Janaya sucked her teeth. We got to the doors and I swiped my ID before taking my stuff off to put through the metal detectors. Janaya took hers off and security stopped her.

"Wait a minute, young-lady. Where's your ID?" he asked her.

"Oh, Cliff. This my little sister. She has an interview here today," I explained.

Janaya reached in her book bag when it came through the other end of the metal detector and took out the letter to show it to him. He nodded his head in approval.

"No parent or guardian is coming with her?" he asked with a raised eye-brow.

I hesitated. "My dad is out of town and our step-mom couldn't miss work so she rode up here with me. She should be cool, though."

Cliff shrugged his shoulders and then pointed to the office. "I guess. Have a seat in there and somebody will be with you."

"Thanks," I said before slapping him a handshake. I walked Janaya to the office.

"Listen, while you're here today, don't think about Pops, or Joselyn, or anything that could be wrong right now. Your grades and your basketball skills already got you here. They just want to see who you are as a person. Just be you and you got this." I coached my sister.

She shrugged. "I guess. But even if I do get in, it's going to suck without you here if you take that early admissions' ticket to USC," Janaya moped.

"You'll be good. Besides, Lamar will still be here." I teased. She blushed harder than she meant to. "See, I knew it. I'm telling."

"Shut up, Dah-Dah!" Janaya yelled as she tried to hide her smile. She walked into the office and I made my way to advisory just as my phone rang. I took a detour to the bathroom instead.

Yani

"Yo Shorty, what's up?" I said to Tashai.

"I didn't hear from you. I was just checking to make sure you weren't mad at me and to make sure you were okay," she replied in a soft voice.

"Oh naw, Shorty. You good. I just got a lot of shit going on right now. My dad ain't come home last night and we haven't heard from him since yesterday morning. This shit ain't like him at all." I explained.

"Yeah, I saw your IG post. I hope he's alright."

"Yeah, me too." I replied.

"Can I see you after school? Will you be able to come keep me company?" she asked sweetly.

I thought about Pops' warning. In light of everything that was going on, I wanted to be some place where I wasn't worried and I knew hanging with Tashai would keep me cool. I was sure Pops would understand.

"I'll be there after practice, all right?" I told her.

"Okay," she said. We said goodbye before hanging up with each other. I then shot Janaya a text telling her to hang out at the library after practice because I would be home late.

I couldn't focus in school. All I could think about was Pops and the message that had been sent to me on Facebook. A part of me wanted to believe that it was just somebody fucking around. Not too many people know that I refer to my dad as "Pops". I looked at the message in my phone again. *"You'll find that nigga where you smell him!"*.

"Mr. Jones, put your phone away. You know better," my English teacher said to me, snapping me out of my thoughts.

I fumbled with my phone before tucking it away in my book bag. "Can I go to the counselor's office? It's an emergency."

The teacher huffed. "The counselor isn't in this week, Davion. What's the problem?"

I looked around the class and noticed everyone was looking at me, which made me feel awkward for the first time in a long time. I was used to being watched, but not at that particular moment. The teacher motioned for me to step out in the hallway when she noticed how uneasy I looked. I briefly explained what was going on with my Dad.

Yani

"Did your family contact the police?" she asked me.

I nodded my head. "But they won't do anything until he's missing for more than twenty-four hours. Anything can happen to him in that time." I hesitated for a moment not sure if I should mention the message. "Last night I posted on Instagram and Facebook asking if anybody had seen him or knew where he was. I got a message this morning from somebody I don't know anything about saying I'll find him where I smell him…"

The English teacher, Ms. Jackson, looked at me startled. "What do you mean? Wait… what?"

"That's what I was just looking at in my phone." I said to her.

"Bring me your phone and show me the message."

I went back into the classroom, which was filled with the hum of pointless conversations, and snatched my phone from my bag.

"Yo Dah-Dah, you good?" Lamar asked me. I put a finger up to let him know to give me a minute before rejoining Ms. Jackson in the hallway. I opened up my Facebook page and showed her the post I put up and then went to the message that was sent to me. Whoever sent it had now deactivated their profile. Ms. Jackson read it and then frowned.

"When did you get this message?" she asked me as she held my phone.

"This morning, right before I left for school," I replied. I was beginning to feel uneasy again.

"Did you tell anybody?"

"Well… no. Because at first I thought it was just somebody being smart, but now I'm not so sure.

Ms. Jackson shook her head as she reached inside of the class and snatched the phone from its cradle on the wall. "You should have shown this to somebody as soon as you got it. Joke or not, assume that it's not a joke… Yes, I need the school police right away." Ms. Jackson put the phone back down and held the door open so I could go back inside of the classroom.

"Pack up your things," she instructed me. "To me, that sounds like a threat or an admission of something ill possibly done to your father and the last thing you should have done was take it lightly.

Yani

The police are going to escort you to the office and ask you some questions. Tell them everything you know, Davion. I know you kids today have that no snitching rule, but this could literally be a life or death situation for your father, do you understand?" she said to me quietly before I made it to my desk.

"Yes," I mumbled. I cursed myself, immediately upset that I would blow off that message like that when I knew better. I fucking knew better! If anything had happened to Pops… I swear, man.

I packed up my book bag just as two school policemen came into the class.

"Is everything all right, Ms. Jackson?" Cliff asked.

"I need you to speak with Davion about something." Ms. Jackson replied, being vague.

"Ay yo, Davion. What's good, yo?" Lamar asked. Suddenly, it was as if I was on center stage with all eyes on me. I was at a loss for words as my head was spinning. "Is your dad cool?"

Other students chimed in as well wondering what was going on. I kept my lips zipped as I thought over what the cops would ask me, what I should and shouldn't tell them and how much more had things gotten fucked up because I didn't say anything about the message sooner.

I followed the cops down to the main office quietly, with my heart racing a mile a minute. I didn't even think about Janaya being in the office when I got down there. Of course, when she saw me being escorted by the police, she jumped up.

"Davion! What's wrong?"

"Sit down, Janaya. I'm cool." I said to her sternly. But the look I gave her let her know something was definitely wrong. Her eyes followed me into the principal's office. Cliff and the other cop closed the door behind us.

"Mr. Jones, I was just telling one of my friends at the Daily News that you were considering taking the early admissions' offer from USC and was setting up an interview for you. Now you're being escorted into my office by the police. What's going on?" the principal asked me.

I looked around at the two cops and then the principal. They all stared back at me intently waiting for me to speak. My nerves were shot and I was feeling sick to my stomach, all the while trying not

Yani

to crack as a feeling deep within the pit of my soul told me my father was not all right. It was the same feeling I got when Janaya told me that Joselyn was on the couch and she couldn't wake her up. I leaned on my knees as flashes from that moment played back in my mind. Taking a deep breath, I looked up at the principal.

"My sister is in the main office. Can she come in here? If she hears this through the grapevine, she's going to snap."

"What's your sister's name?"

"Janaya Jones," I said in return. The principal nodded for Cliff to bring her in the room.

Cliff opened the door and stepped half-way out. "Janaya Jones?" Jah-Jah looked up at him and he waved her in his direction. She grabbed her book bag and walked nervously over to the office.

"Janaya, sit down," I said to her.

"No. I don't want to sit down. What's wrong with my dad?" she asked as she stared at me.

I shook my head as I looked at the floor. I then told the principal and officers about my dad not coming home and how we couldn't get him on the phone or a response from him through texting. They suggested I try calling him again. I called from the phone in the office but again it went straight to voice mail.

"Same crap from yesterday." I said as I placed the phone back in its cradle. I then explained how Meagan called the cops but was told we had to wait until he had been missing for twenty-four hours before they could do anything, so I took it upon myself to post on Facebook and Instagram to get more people looking for him or at least turn up some information.

"Then this morning, I was about to leave for school when I got a message on Facebook from somebody saying we would find him where we smelled him," I said. I looked at the floor. The room fell silent as though everyone was trying to make sure they heard me correctly. "I didn't say anything because I thought it was just somebody being nutty. But now… I don't know."

Janaya spoke first. "You didn't tell Meagan when you got that message? That was almost two hours ago, Davion!" she yelled. Before I knew it, Janaya had stormed over to me and slapped the bullshit out of me. I didn't even know my sister had hands like that. In fact, she made my lip bleed. I

Yani

jumped out of my seat, not intending to hit her, but out of reflex. Cliff grabbed me thinking I was going to hit her back.

"Somebody told you Pops was dead and you waited two hours, Davion! Two hours!" she screamed as she hit me in my chest. Tears spilled from her eyes and I felt like a complete dickhead.

"I'm sorry, Jah! I didn't think they were serious… I didn't... I'm sorry!" I said back to her. My sister looked crushed as she held her hands to her face crying. I wanted to hug her but Cliff was still holding me back. The principal put his hand on her shoulder and squeezed gently as a way to comfort her.

"Can you let me go, Cliff? I wasn't going to hit her. Let me go, man." I said calmly. The principal nodded for him to release his hold on me and I grabbed Janaya. She resisted me at first but I held her anyway. "I'm sorry, Jah-Jah. I'm sorry." I told her as I stroked the back of her head.

"We need your phone," Cliff said to me. I pointed to my book bag. When he pulled it out, I gave him the pin number without hesitation to unlock my phone and he went to my Facebook messages. When he saw the message, he showed it to the other officer and the principal.

Before I knew it, Janaya and I were being taken from the school to the nearby police station on Broad and Champlost. I was being grilled with questions about Pops' associates, hobbies, his job, potential enemies and everything else. An hour after we had been at the station, Meagan showed up. They must have told her about the message because if looks could kill, the way she looked at me, I would have been a dead ass.

After getting Pops' information about the supermarket he owned as well as the make, model, and plates to his car, the cops finally let us go. We walked back to Meagan's car in silence. I was on pins and needles wondering when she was going to unload on me. Shockingly, she didn't.

"You should have told me about that message as soon as you got it this morning, Davion. Every minute counts. Every second." She shook her head as she drove. "I'm not mad that you brushed it off because I know people are ass-holes, even in situations like this. I'm just mad that you didn't tell me so we could've gotten a jump on this before they deleted their profile."

I was all out of apologies and hated feeling like I was the bad guy. Shit, there were things that she knew that she wasn't saying anything about, so who really was the bad guy?

The shit hit the news mad quick. But for whatever reason, the news segment wasn't about a missing husband and father, but instead was about a star athlete from Central who could possibly be on his way to USC on an early admissions' ticket with a full scholarship, whose father had gone missing. I swear, mainstream media is so fucking twisted. This shit wasn't about me. It was about getting information on his whereabouts and bringing my dad home safe and sound.

I don't know how my number got out, but before I knew it, I was getting calls from reporters wanting to interview me. They were even showing up at the fucking house. The shit was ridiculous. By Thursday, I had snapped when I was putting the trash out and one walked up on me.

"Y'all focused on the wrong shit. I'm not worried about no fucking scholarship to USC right now and my dad's been missing for more than two days. Why y'all not out looking for him instead of putting cameras and microphones in my face, asking me about shit that ain't fucking important to me right now?" I hissed.

"Davion, no disrespect to your father, but a junior getting this kind of invite to USC is unheard of and big news. And to be honest, it would get more people to pay attention to the story of your father missing as well as get our audience's sympathy. You may not like it, but it's business and could be beneficial to him and you," the reporter explained.

I looked at him for a moment, partially understanding what he was saying, but still not liking it. I shrugged, giving in. He let out a sigh of relief.

"Just two questions and I promise, I'll be out of your way," he said with a hopeful expression. I nodded my head. "Great! Davion, have you decided whether or not you'll take USC up on their offer and what does an opportunity like this mean to you and your family.

I took a page from the reporter's slimy book. "Right now, my main focus is locating my dad and making sure he's okay. You know, while this might be a dope opportunity for me, since USC is where I really wanted to go anyway, I'm more concerned with my father and my family, so no decision will be made until this business is squared away."

The reporter nodded his head with a smile, recognizing what I did. I went back into the house and closed the door. Meagan was on her phone, but she didn't look pleased with the conversation. I walked over to her and waited for her to finish.

"Okay… thank you for that update. Yes, sir… yes. Okay… thanks again… goodbye." She disconnected the call but stared at her phone. My heart was in my throat wondering what the update was.

"What?" I finally asked.

Meagan shook her head. "They found his car. The keys were still inside, in the ignition," she said in a quiet voice.

"That's not good," I thought to myself. "Where did they find it?" I asked instead.

"Near Rising Sun and Adams Ave," she told me. "They said there were a few splatters of blood on the door. They're waiting to find out if it's his or not and are searching the area for him…" she trailed off before turning abruptly to the side and vomiting.

"Meagan… you good?" I asked. I pulled a chair out so she could sit down.

"I just found out I'm pregnant, Davion." She shook her head. "I haven't even had the chance to tell him, yet."

"Fuck…" I thought. "Don't talk like you won't get to tell him. You will." I said to her confidently even though inside, something told me that she wouldn't.

I checked the time on my phone and saw that King was about to let out. I didn't go to school that day, not wanting to deal with the endless questions and people staring at me. But I wanted to see Tashai.

"I'll be back." I said to Meagan.

"Where are you going?" she asked me.

I hesitated. "I was going to meet Lamar at his house so I could get the homework I missed. I won't be gone long." I lied.

"Call me as soon as you get there. Tell Jah-Jah to come straight home." Meagan said firmly.

Yani

I nodded my head as I grabbed my jacket and left out the house. I ran to the bus stop and got there just as the 18 was coming. I jumped on it quickly and jumped off just as the XH was pulling up at Washington Lane and Chew Avenue. I made it over to King just as Tashai was coming out of the building with a couple of her friends.

"Hey," I said to her.

She smiled at me before I gave her a hug. I peeped how her friends were checking me out.

"I'll see y'all later," she said to her friends as I put my arm over her shoulder.

"Oh, I see how you do. You ain't low. I thought you were coming to Trenda's house?" one of her friends asked.

Tashai laughed as I pulled her away. We began walking back to the XH bus stop. Two buses passed us by, so we decided to just walk to her house since it wasn't too far. I could tell she wanted to ask me about the situation with my dad but wasn't sure if she should.

"Did you decide if you would take USC up on their offer?" she asked me.

I sighed. "That seems to be the hot topic right now."

"Yeah, it's been all on the news."

I shook my head. "Yeah, they should be talking about my dad and how he's been missing for more than two days but instead, they're geeking about this shit. I don't even know if I want to go, now."

"What? Why wouldn't you? It's a great opportunity," Tashai asked as she looked at me surprised.

"I'm just not worried about it right now. Talk about something else," I told her.

"Okay… like what?" she asked.

"Like how you been ducking me," I said in return.

Tashai laughed. "Ducking you how?"

"I'm trying to wife you and you hitting the matrix pass all that shit." We both chuckled.

"No I'm not. Plus, you got all these other chicks out here you talking to."

"What? I ain't talking to nobody else. Where you get your info from?" I asked as I looked at her. Tashai shrugged her shoulders. "Yo, if I wasn't into you like that, I wouldn't have came all the way from my crib in Cedarbrook to King with these crazy niggas out here so I could meet you at y'all let out and then walk you home. It's cold as shit out here, too!" We chuckled again and then Tashai became quiet.

"I just want to make sure I'm the girl you want and not just the girl you're curious about. Then when that curiosity is satisfied, you dip out on me," she said finally.

I nodded my head. "I feel you. But it ain't like that. Trust me. I like you, Shorty. You got a good head on your shoulders and you ain't out here thotting like some of these other jawns. I'm tryna learn more about you and see where we can go from there. Just stop ducking me."

Tashai fell silent as we approached her house. I waited while she unlocked the door and we went inside.

"Do you want something to eat or drink?" she asked as she hung up her coat.

"Nah, I ate before I came to meet you." My phone went off. I looked at it and saw it was a call from Meagan. I started to answer it but sent it to my voicemail figuring if it was important, she would leave a message.

Hoop Dreams Deflated

Tashai did her homework while we talked about sports, politics and music. Man, she was smart. I could listen to her talk all day. The way she talked about our community, the state of it and the way it could be fixed by starting with group economics and keeping the Black dollar in the Black community by supporting Black businesses and rebuilding Black Wall Street had me blown away.

"Let me chill. You probably think I'm weird, now." She chuckled nervously as she put her books back in her book bag.

"Nah, not at all. Like I said, you got a good head on your shoulders. Not a lot of chicks your age on your level, mentally. You kinda remind me of Tupac." I told her.

Tashai laughed. "Yeah, it's a reason why they killed him which is much deeper than gangsta rap. That man was wise beyond his years."

She sat next to me on the couch and began picking her nails. The silence was weird. I wondered what she was thinking. I smiled to myself as I thought of doing something corny.

Yani

"Hold up, I need to make a call." I said as I pulled my phone from my pocket.

"Oh okay," she said softly. I was hoping she asked who I was calling.

"Let me call my girl, real quick." I said with a straight face.

"Your… your girl? Your girlfriend?" she stuttered. I could detect the fire in her as I began dialing a number. She was about to say something but I put a finger up to silence her.

My Boo by Alicia Keys and Usher came on and Tashai jumped. She picked her phone up from the coffee table and looked at it before looking at me.

"You play all day," she said with a grin as she answered it.

"My boo, huh?" I said into the phone. She burst out laughing, falling back into the couch. I disconnected the call and sat next to her. "That's how you feel?" I asked her.

"What's my ring tone on your phone?" she asked as she peered at me.

"Call it and find out," I told her as I leaned back on the couch. She dialed my number and waited. *Take Care* by Drake and Rihanna came on.

"Awww," she blushed.

"So, you still ducking me or naw?" I asked her.

"I said I wasn't ducking you." Tashai replied. I motioned for her to come to me and she scooted closer. I couldn't wait to kiss her. Her kiss brought me peace even with everything going on with Pops and Meagan, and having to give USC my decision the next day. Feeling her that close to me calmed me and in that moment, made me believe that everything would be okay. I needed her. It was the first time I had ever felt that way about a girl.

Our make-out session became more intense and my hands began to explore her body. I felt her tense up and then she jerked away.

"What's wrong?" I asked. She scooted away from me and stared at the floor for a moment before closing her eyes. I reached out to touch her shoulder to see if she was okay and she jumped, causing me to snatch my hand away.

"I'm sorry," she apologized. She stood up and began pulling on her shirt as though she was trying to cover her body though she wasn't revealing herself. What the hell happened to her?

"It's okay..." I tried to say to her but she shook her head rapidly.

Yani

"No... it's not." An awkward silence infiltrated the living room. I stood up and grabbed my coat.

"I've gotta get Jah-Jah from the library. Can I call you later?" I asked her. She nodded her head but still wouldn't look at me. I kissed her on the cheek before leaving and could tell how tense she was. I didn't know what was up with her, but I'd hoped that she could trust me enough to tell me what it was. I'd also hoped it wasn't a case where someone had hurt her. I got a text from Meagan telling me she picked Janaya up from the library and to bring my ass straight from wherever I was. She seemed pissed.

I left Tashai's house and went straight home. When I got in, Meagan went off.

"Where were you?" she yelled when I came in the house.

"I told you, I was going to Lamar's house to get the homework I missed.

"Boy, don't stand here and lie to me. I called your phone and you didn't answer. I called over to Ms. Aretha's house only for her to say you never showed up. With everything going on, do you know how got-damn worried I was?" Meagan snapped.

I didn't know what to say. That was the first time Meagan had ever gone off on me. "I'm sorry…" was all I could think to say.

"Save the sorry shit, Davion," she said to me as she put her hand up to silence me. "Where the hell were you?" she asked me again.

"I was with my girlfriend, Tashai."

Meagan looked at me as though I were crazy. She then punched me in my chest. "Have you lost your damned mind? Your father has been missing for almost three days and you declined my call so you could lay up with some damn girl? Are you serious?" she hissed as she hit me in the chest again.

"Man, I'm not sticking around for this," I said as I turned away. Meagan snatched me by my shirt and yanked me back to her.

"Oh no, your ass will stick around and you better not move," she sneered at me. I shook my head refusing to look at her. Not out of disrespect, but out of frustration and hurt. "Your father could be dead."

"You don't know that he is," I said to her.

"And you don't know that he isn't. I can NOT handle losing you or Janaya. You two are like my own kids so if I ask you to come straight home or stay in the house until we figure out what the hell is going on, fucking humor me!"

"Fine…" I murmured. She let my shirt go.

"I know you were holding off on giving your decision because of what's going on with your dad. But I know your father wouldn't want you to pass up on this opportunity, no matter how things turn out with him. So tomorrow, accept their early admissions' invitation, okay?"

I looked at Meagan confused for a moment. To me, it seemed like she had already given up and presumed my father was dead. I nodded my head and then made my way up to my room. I peeked my head into Janaya's room first.

"You good?" I asked her.

"Yeah, I'm straight," she replied blandly. Janaya hadn't said much to me since she found out about the message that had been sent to me.

"You still mad at me?" I asked her. She shook her head at me as she continued to watch the old episode of *Martin* where he and Gina were at Chilligan's Island fighting the big rat. I watched for a second. "I love you, Jah-Jah," I said to her in a sappy voice. She looked at me and I gave her my big, sad puppy eyes. She burst out laughing.

"Get out my room, Dah-Dah. You so irking!"

"You talk to your little boyfriend?" I teased her.

"Oh my God!" she shrieked before grabbing her big, oversized teddy bear from Six Flag's Great Adventure and throwing it at me. "You get on my nerves!"

"Janaya and Lamar sitting in a tree," I sang. She jumped from the bed and ran to push me out of the door.

"Shut up!" she yelled before closing the door on me. I made kissing noises from outside of her door and we both burst out laughing. I love that little girl. She's my twin minus three years.

That night I laid in my bed staring up at the ceiling. I thought back to the first night I slept in this room and how Pops schooled me on my hygiene and other things. For some reason, I reached for the lamp and turned it on, watching the dinosaurs move about across my ceiling. I wondered where Pops was, if he was okay or if he was in pain. I prayed that he wasn't suffering and

Yani

his absence just stemmed from some business that he was taking care of that he didn't want us involved in. I prayed that he came home soon. Our lives would never be the same without him.

The next morning, I woke up feeling refreshed with a positive outlook on life. I couldn't wait to get to school so I could give the counselor my decision and have my roster updated. The coach informed me that the extra classes I would be taking would be at night on Mondays, Wednesdays and Fridays at what they called "Twilight" school. Friday classes would be online which was perfect because we never had games on that day.

Before I took care of things with the counselor, I wanted to check on Tashai. I called her as I stopped at Dunkin Donuts to get a bagel and a juice.

"Good morning," she answered, sounding like her usual self. Her cheerful voice threw me for a loop.

"Hey bae, good morning." I said back as I paid for my breakfast. "How you feeling this morning?"

"I'm good. About to get off the bus and head to school," she said back.

"Everything straight with you? Because yesterday…"

She interrupted me. "Not right now, Davion."

I hesitated and there was a brief moment of silence. "You can talk to me about anything, alright? So, if it's something wrong…"

She interrupted me again. "We can talk after school."

"Okay…" I hopped on the 18 bus to ride back to Central. "So, listen, I decided to take USC up on their offer." I told her as I made my way to the back of the bus.

"Really! That's what's up, Davion!" she said. Tashai sounded just as excited as I was.

"Yeah, I can't wait. I'll let you know how that goes after school. But real quick before I go into the building; are we making this official or naw?"

"Yes," she said to me and for some reason, I could almost tell she was blushing.

"Alright, alright. So that means you have a boyfriend, now."

"And that means you have a girlfriend now," she said in return.

Yani

"I'ma see you after school. Maybe we can go to the movies or something."

"Okay. I'm about to head into school," Tashai said quickly.

"Yeah, me too. I'ma holla at you when I get out."

"Okay." I disconnected the call and went through the metal detectors. When I saw Cliff, I slapped him a handshake.

"Today's the big day. Did you decide?" he asked me as I walked through the detector.

"Yeah, I'm about to head to the counselor now to let him know," I said with a huge grin.

"You gon' let me know now or do I have to wait for the press conference?" Cliff asked before laughing. I laughed with him.

"I ain't gon' do you like that," I told him. I happened to look up the hall and saw the counselor huddled with two of the other school police officers. One of them came over to Cliff and pulled him to the side. They talked in a hushed tone. I couldn't tell what it was about because Cliff had the greatest Poker face ever.

"Mr. Hamilton!" I called to the counselor.

"He has some things to take care of, Davion. Come down during your lunch break, okay?" Cliff said quickly.

"Damn!" I thought to myself. I grabbed my book bag and headed over to my locker. I saw some of the guys from the basketball team as well as some of the other guys I was cool with. Not to brag, but I was one of the most popular guys in school. Walking up and down the hallway was a non-stop hand shake and fist dap session sometimes. Of course, the shorties showed me love too, but I only had one girl I was thinking about.

I got to my first period English class feeling anxious like shit. I couldn't wait to tell the counselor what my decision was and get things rolling. A part of me feared the unknown while another part of me couldn't wait to embrace it. Lamar tapped me on my shoulder.

"Yo bro," he spoke as he took a seat next to me.

I slapped him a handshake. "What's up, Mar?"

"So, you going?" he asked me with a raised eyebrow.

Yani

I nodded my head. "Yeah. I'm rolling. I was going to tell the counselor this morning but Cliff told me he had some other things to take care of and to come back during lunch."

"That's what's up," Lamar said as he slapped me another handshake. He looked a little sad. Despite the fact that he stood off to the side while I was getting jumped all those years back, he remained my closest best friend. He also showed that he learned from that incident because since then, he's always had my back.

"That means when you become a Hoya, I'ma have to embarrass ya ass on the courts," I joked to lighten the mood. When he moved on to Georgetown, which was his top pick, that would be the first time since we were thirteen that we would be opponents. We always played on the same team since then.

Ms. Jackson was writing out the lesson on the board when someone knocked on the classroom door. She went over to it to see who it was. I took out my homework from the night before and began writing down the notes from the board. She lingered at the door for a bit and then came back inside. Whoever that was at the door must have said something she didn't like because she looked like someone had just broken her heart. She stalled for a minute before going back to writing on the board. When she finished, she sat down at her desk and put her hands together, intertwining her fingers as though she was praying. I didn't know what was up with her, but whatever it was, I hoped she was okay.

Ms. Jackson looked up and caught me staring at her. She offered a nervous smile and then cleared her throat.

"Class, please be sure that your phones and tablets are turned off. Do not silence the ringer or put it on vibrate. Turn them completely off," she instructed us, which was a first. I had already turned mine off from when I talked to Tashai before coming in the building.

"Oh shit…" I heard Lamar mumble next to me as he looked at his phone.

"Language, Mr. Pearson." Ms. Jackson said sternly.

"Sor… sorry Ms. Jackson." Lamar apologized as he looked at his phone. He turned it off and then looked at me. I shot him a look as though to ask what was up, but he looked stumped.

Yani

We got down to work with the day's lesson being on Paul Laurence Dunbar's poetry. The piece of his that we were interpreting was *"We Wear the Mask"*. After reading it, Ms. Jackson asked if anyone wanted to give their interpretation. Nobody raised their hand, so I did.

"Yes, Mr. Jones." Ms. Jackson said as she pointed to me.

"I think the poem is talking about frauds," I said aloud. Some of the classmates snickered. "Naw, listen. I don't mean like frauds where people pretend to be something for likes like on social media. I mean, people wear masks to hide who they are for different reasons. Everybody has a mask. Most people wear it because they have ill intentions. Some people wear a mask because they don't' want people to see what's hurting them. Either way it's frauding, but sometimes wearing a mask is necessary." I said.

Ms. Jackson nodded her head. She was about to add on to what I said to her when the loud speaker came on.

"Davion Jones, please report to the main office. Davion Jones, please report to the main office."

Everyone looked at me wondering what I was being summoned for. I suspected it was about my decision with USC. I looked over at Ms. Jackson.

"Do I need a pass?" I asked. She shook her head at me. I shrugged my shoulders and got up from my seat.

"Take your things with you…" she said softly.

I turned back around and grabbed my book bag, quickly putting my things inside. I happened to glance at Lamar and noticed his head was down. I made a mental note to talk to him during lunch about my USC decision, to let him know we would still be home boys and who knows, maybe he would change his mind and come to USC with me the following year.

I left the class and made my way down to the office. My nerves were everywhere as I prepared to let the counselor and the principal know that I was taking USC up on their offer. I never got a chance to give my decision though.

I stood in the principal's office unable to hear anything else he was saying after he told me that they found my father's body in Tacony Creek late last night and had positively identified his body that morning. I stare at the principal, seeing his mouth moving but not hearing the words coming out. I was numb and cold at the same time. How is that possible? If the body is numb, I shouldn't feel cold, right? At least that's what I was thinking at the moment.

"Has anyone told my sister?" I asked the principal.

He shook his head. "Your step mother is on her way here to pick you up. Your family has my deepest condolences and sympathies. If there is anything that this school or myself can do during this difficult time, we will do it. Also, in light of this tragedy, we are extending the time frame for you to give your decision while you…"

"No," I said, interrupting him.

"I'm sorry?" the principal replied as he looked at me confused.

"I don't need an extension. I'm not going." I told him.

"Davion, I understand you are hurting right now, which is why now isn't the best time for you to make this decision."

"Mr. Valdez, I don't give a fuck about USC right now, sorry. My father was just found dead in a fucking creek not too far from where we live. My sister and I found my mother dead in our house of a drug over dose a few years ago. Fuck USC!" I hissed.

Mr. Valdez insisted on arguing his point but Cliff waved him off.

"I'll talk to him," Cliff told him.

"Nah, ain't nothing to talk about." I said as I bolted upward from my seat. I paced back and forth in the office trying my damndest not to shed any tears in front of them. I didn't want to share my grief. I needed to be strong and make sure that Janaya was okay. As a matter of fact, I didn't want anyone telling her but me.

"Tell me what you need." Cliff said to me.

I couldn't think. The more I paced, the harder it was to breathe and the harder it was to think. I shook my head as I breathed heavily.

"I don't want my sister to find out from nobody but me. Can you call her school and tell them to put her in the office? Take her phone and don't turn on the news."

"Done," Cliff said as he picked up the phone. "Yes, this is officer Cliff at Central High School. I

Yani

need Janaya Jones to be brought to the main office immediately. Keep her isolated, make sure you take her phone and there is no news or radio on. Her father's body was just found and her brother doesn't want her to have to hear it from anyone but him… Thank you."

As soon as Cliff hung up the phone, I kicked over a chair and flipped the principal's desk. I punched my fist into the wall, breaking it, but I didn't feel it. The pain from losing my mother and my father was too great. I hollered out, sounding like a wounded animal in the cold streets, which is very close to what I felt like. Cliff grabbed me and hugged me, but I continued to holler.

Word must have spread because before I knew it, damn near the entire basketball team had squeezed into the nurse's office, who bandaged my hand to briefly hold me over until I could get to the hospital. They had me surrounded, with all of them hugging me. Lamar held me the tightest and shed tears along with me. That's why he had the outburst in class while he was turning his phone off. He saw the bulletin from NBC 10 News on his phone. There was a lot of love in that room that day. But it would never substitute the love I received from my father.

Meagan was in the waiting room when I finally managed to get out of the nurse's office. The counselor was rubbing her back and giving her tissue after tissue. When she saw me, she burst into tears before grabbing me and holding me tightly. I was signed out of school and we went to her car.

I hadn't been driving long. Pops had taken me out a few times to drive but I had my permit. Meagan was in no position to drive, so I took the keys and drove over to Janaya's school. I wasn't prepared to break this news to her. But it had to be done.

I took a deep breath and wiped my face and eyes as best as I could before walking into the building. After signing the visitor's sheet, I went to the office and saw Janaya sitting in the principal's office. The secretary pointed for me to go in.

"Jah-Jah…" I said with my voice cracking.

She turned around and looked at me smiling when she heard my voice. But when she saw my face, her smile faded. I bit my bottom lip as I shook my head at her.

Yani

"Pops…?" she said softly.

I continued shaking my head not knowing what to say. She looked down and then put her hands to her face. I knelt in front of her and put my arms around her as she fell to her knees.

"Dah-Dah!" she cried. "Why? Like, why Dah-Dah? First mom, now Pops!"

I didn't know what to say to her to console her. Both of our parents were gone. If there really was a God, how could he be this cold to leave two kids parentless? How could he be so cold that he could let them both get taken out like this?

Despite me insisting that I was okay and my hand was fine, Meagan made me go to Einstein hospital to get my hand placed in a cast. Pops was dead, and there was no way in hell I was going to sit in the E.R at Einstein all fucking day. I drove to Chestnut Hill Hospital instead, knowing they wouldn't take nearly as long.

I was still in disbelief over the news of Pops' murder. Who would want to hurt him? I shook my head against that question, feeling stupid, knowing that when you're in the street pharmacy business, enemies and friends sometimes wear the same mask… *We wear the mask…*

Hoop Dreams Deflated

My phone was popping. Text messages, Facebook inboxes, tweets, Instagram messages and phone calls had my phones constantly humming in my bag. I didn't want to talk to anybody. I wanted to be back in my bed, looking up at the ceiling watching the dinosaurs intersect one another as they moved about. I wanted Pops to peek his head in my room before he went to bed to tell me goodnight and remind me that the day was done. No matter what troubles occurred, brush them off and embrace the new day ahead. "Ignore what you can't conquer, conquer what you can't ignore," is what he always would say to me.

My hand was set and placed in a cast. I was given a prescription for Percocet and sent home. I stuffed the script in my bag, doubting that I was ever going to use that shit.

"Everything is finished?" Meagan asked me. She looked extremely tired as though she had aged five years in the last five hours.

"Yeah," I mumbled. Her and Janaya stood up so we could leave.

Walking into the house was weird as shit. Even though Pops was never coming home again,

Yani

I could still feel his presence in the house. But at the same time, his physical absence could be felt and it left me feeling sick.

None of us said anything, we were all in our own heads trying to process the news of his murder. Janaya went straight up to her room and slammed her door. Meagan retreated to the kitchen and began cooking. I stood in the living room staring blankly. I felt empty inside but was too hurt to cry.

"I need some fucking air," I said before turning towards the front door. I thought Meagan was going to stop me, but shockingly, she didn't.

Since I still had her key ring on my finger, I hopped back in the car and drove to Tashai's house. Before I had a chance to ring the door bell, she was opening the front door. She grabbed me and hugged me.

"I'm sorry…" she said softly as she rubbed the back of my head. "I'm so, so, sorry, Davion."

"Thank you," I murmured as I held her.

She let me go and stepped aside so I could come in her house. "I tried calling you and texting you when word got around at school, but you weren't answering. Then I was worried that everybody knew but you…"

"Nah, I found out this morning in school. The principal called me into his office to tell me," I explained to her as I sat on the sofa.

"Dang, what happened to your hand?" she asked as she stood near me.

I looked at my hand in the thick, hard cast. It dawned on me it was my dribbling hand. "Fuck…" I cursed out loud as I shook my head. That meant I was automatically out for the rest of the season. "I broke it punching the wall." I put my good hand to my face as I stared down at the floor. This shit couldn't be happening. After all of my hard work to get this far, only to be set back because Pops wanted to live a lifestyle that would cost him his life and fuck up ours. Did he not pay attention to how fucked up shit was when we were little and living with Joselyn? And that was because of him! Ultimately, all of our lives had been changed or damaged one way or another because he wanted to be a fucking trap king. What if my hand doesn't heal properly and my scholarship to USC gets taken as well as any potential offers during my senior year? I had never bothered to come up with a backup plan because this was my plan! Nothing was going to stand in my way and I made that vow as I sat starving in the living room of Joselyn's house while the roaches crypt-walked up and down the fucking walls!

At that moment, I wanted to have an entire Boyz N' Da Hood moment where Tre' started swinging at the air. But I didn't want to swing at the air, I wanted to swing on Pops. I wanted to kick his fucking ass for not thinking ahead, for not understanding the street life only had two ways out for most people; death or jail. I wanted to kick his fucking ass for using us as an excuse to get into this dead-end-ass life instead of letting us be the reason for him to stay far the fuck away from it!

Tashai placed her hand on the back of my head and I leaned my head against her stomach for comfort. I didn't want to cry in front of her because I didn't want to look like a weak-ass nut. But I was fucking hurt and I was angry.

"What the fuck are we going to do, now?" I groaned, becoming choked up. Tashai held me tighter and that shit caused me to ball my fucking eyes out. Joselyn was gone, Pops was gone, my dreams of being an NBA All Star, Championship winning MVP, Olympic Gold Medalist was probably gone, too. I felt a sickening sense of fear; fear of the unknown as far as where my future was headed, because this was the first time I couldn't see it since I dribbled a basketball the very first time. That fear mixed together with anguish and sorrow like an emotional concoction and I trembled like a leaf that was a gentle breeze's whisper away from being ripped from its' branch. The branch was my hopes and dreams and I was the leaf.

Tashai sniffed and I looked up at her, noticing that she was crying, too. It then dawned on me that just earlier this year, her father had been murdered as well. That was not a commonality that any two teenagers should have had to share.

"I'm sorry, Shorty. I ain't mean to get you worked up, too." I apologized as I reached up to wipe her face.

She shook her head. "It's cool. I'm just glad I can be here for you like this because when my dad was killed, nobody was really there for me, and I was more focused on making sure my mom didn't fall apart. So, I never even really got to grieve like that."

I shook my head also. "This is too fucked up."

Tashai nodded her head as to agree with me. "Yeah. You sound just like me when my dad was killed."

"Your dad sold drugs?" I asked bluntly.

Tashai shook her head. "No, but he hung with some shady people and when they got pulled out on, he was with them and they ended up killing him. The crazy thing is, they weren't even looking for him and not only that, the ones that they were looking for didn't even get shot. My dad caught almost every bullet and died before he hit the ground…" Tashai trailed off as she put her hand to her mouth before bursting into tears. This was too fucking much. I opened my mouth to say something to comfort her but she held a finger up to silence me. Her mouth opened to say something else but the look on her face suggested that her next statement was filled with a pain I could never describe. "While my father was being killed, his brother was molesting me!" she finally said as her voice wavered. I stared up at her in shock. I then thought back to the night before when we were making out in her house and she froze up. I was really hoping that something like this wasn't the reason.

"I never told my mom," she said as she began to calm down while wiping her face with the back of her hands.

"Why?" I asked.

"How could I? With the pain of her husband getting gunned down just around the corner from our house… can you imagine what it would have done to her if she found out not only what had happened to me, but when it happened?" she explained.

"So, you sacrificed yourself to spare her," I concluded. Tashai thought on my words and then smirked at the truth and irony behind them. "Is that why you don't like being in here by yourself?"

"Sometimes," she said softly. We fell silent at that moment. I leaned back on the couch and pulled her on top of me so she could lay on my chest. As I stroked her hair, I thought of Janaya and felt like shit. I needed to be there for her right now just as much, if not more, than I was for Tashai.

Yani

After ten minutes or more had gone by with us just lying in silence, I looked at my watch.

"Babe, I need to go check on my step-mom and my sister. I know Jah-Jah gotta be going through it right now." I told her.

Tashai sat up and I sat up with her. "You want me to walk you to the bus stop?" she asked me.

"Nah, I got my step-mom's car. I'ma call you later. It's probably a bunch of people at the house. I'm not even in the mood, honestly." I said as I got up and stretched.

"I didn't know you could drive," Tashai said as she walked me to the door.

"Yeah, one day I'ma have to come scoop you up," I smiled. I hugged her tightly and held her for a moment, not so much for my benefit, but for hers as well. "I'll call you later."

"Okay. It doesn't matter how late, I'll be up. I'm here for you," she told me.

"I appreciate that, Shorty," I said as I leaned in to kiss her. She didn't hesitate or tense up. Hopefully getting that off her chest did her some good. I knew that one day she would have to tell her mom what happened and get some type of help. Mentally and emotionally, that's way too much baggage for any one person to carry.

I hopped in Meagan's car and let it warm up for a second. I noticed Tashai was still standing in the doorway watching me. When I was ready to drive away, I honked the horn at her. She waved at me and I pulled off so I could go home and face the aftermath of my father's murder.

I could barely find parking when I got back to the block. Maybe it was because I was the one driving and looking for parking, but I could never remember a time in the eleven years that we lived on that block that it was packed like this. Not even during the summer.

I managed to find a spot that someone was pulling out of, after circling the block, that wasn't too far from the house. After pulling in, I walked over to the house and noticed there were quite a few people there.

"Oh my God! Davion!" my aunt yelped when she saw me come through the door. She was my father's older sister who I only saw when she wanted money from him. Tears streamed out of her eyes as she grabbed me and hugged me. She

Yani

bellowed in my ear, which annoyed the fuck out of me. I managed to keep a Poker face… like Cliff's. Aunt Regine let me go and looked at me before crying out again. "You look so much like your father, I swear that man could have spit you out himself. Mmh mmh MMH!!" she shook her head before dabbing at her eyes with a tissue. Buck and Sam were off in a corner talking to Meagan. Their gathering looked a little too secretive. I wanted to butt in on their conversation, but my aunts, uncles and some of Pops' friends kept stopping me to tell me how much I looked like Cortez and hitting me with the "I remember when" and the "Remember that time…" "No the fuck I don't," is what I wanted to yell at them along with a few "Get the fuck outta my face" and "Y'all niggas phony as fuck," but I managed to hold my tongue. *We wear the mask…* It's funny how that poem from the day's English class lesson turned out to be my theme for the day.

I managed to escape and make my way over to Meagan, Buck and Sam. Sam noticed me coming and cleared his throat. He wasn't low at all.

Buck shook my hand. "Young bol, my condolences. Your pops' been my right-hand man since we were balling at Gratz back in the day."

"Thanks," I said as I peered at all of them. Something felt off. I could feel it in the air like that Beanie Sigel song.

"I heard you're headed to USC early," Sam said to me.

I shook my head. "I declined. I'ma finish out my junior and senior year. Plus, I fucked my hand up so…" I glanced at Meagan to see if she would check me for cursing, but she didn't. That was odd.

"Damn young bol, that would've been a helluva opportunity for you." Buck said to me. I shrugged him off.

"Where were you when Pops dropped off the radar?" I asked him as I looked him straight in the eye.

"Davion…" Meagan said as she gave me a sharp look. I shot the same one back to her and then looked back at Buck.

"What'chu tryna' say?" Buck asked me back.

"I'm saying, you said my pops was your right-hand man since way back when. He's normally with you when he ain't at the store, the shop or home. So, what happened?"

Buck looked offended but fuck his offense. I didn't like the way they were huddled up over here while my peoples were stopping by to pay their respects, and I damn sure didn't like the way they changed up when I came over to them.

"Outta respect for your pops, I'ma act like I don't peep how you tryna say I let him get snatched up, because you a little nigga that don't know shit about what was going on. Stick to basketball, a'ight." Buck said to me in a low, menacing tone. If Pops were here, he never would've had the heart to talk to me like that.

"Okay, you guys need to chill out, okay. We're not doing this here. We're not doing this at all." Meagan said as she looked at all of us. "Davion, your sister hasn't come out of her room since we came home. Go check on her to make sure she's all right."

I looked at Meagan for a moment and then went upstairs like she said. Something was up and I was going to find the fuck out sooner than later.

I tapped lightly on Janaya's door but she didn't answer. I figured maybe she didn't hear me, so I knocked a little louder. When she still didn't say anything, I opened her door.

"Jah-Jah?" I called to her. She was laying across her bed with one of Pop's hooded sweat shirts on, holding her pillow close to her. I went over to her and sat on the side of her bed.

"If you're in here to tell me to come downstairs to sit with all those fake-ass people, get the hell out of my room. If you're here to tell me everything will be okay, shut the hell up and get the hell out of my room. And don't even think about giving me some dumb-ass speech about Pops being in a better place, because I don't want to hear it." Janaya said angrily. Each word dripped with more venom and held more contempt than its previous. I usually hated when she cursed, but I understood her pain, frustration, sorrow and anger more than anyone, so I let it slide.

I sighed as I looked at her. "No… I just wanted to make sure you were okay."

Janaya cut her eyes at me. "Do I look okay?"

I didn't know what to say to that, so I fell silent for a moment. Janaya then burst into tears. But her cries held a pain that was agonizing to me.

Yani

Comforting her should have been easy since she was my little sister, but I didn't know how at that moment. Apart of me felt guilty for not saying anything when I received that Facebook message, and I wondered if she blamed me. I wasn't sure if it would have made a difference or not, if I had said something about it sooner, but now we would never know.

Janaya sat up and then rested her head in my lap. I stroked her hair as my mind went back to the SD card I had taken from Pops' room.

"You hungry?" I asked Janaya.

She shook her head. "I'm not going downstairs while all those people are down there," she told me.

"I'll get something for you. You gotta eat something or you're going to get sick. I'll be right back." I said as I got up from her bed. I left her room and then went back to mine.

I closed my bedroom door and sat down with my MacBook. After retrieving the SD card from my book bag, I played with it between my fingers feeling nervous. Butterflies danced around my stomach as I wondered what was on the card and why Pops would hide it in his headboard. I stuck it inside of my laptop and waited nervously for it to open. When it did, I noticed it was a bunch of recorded files along with some Microsoft Excel documents. All of the files were either encrypted or had a password attached to them. I tried opening one anyway, only to come across a message about security from Vivint.

"What the hell was Vivint?" I thought to myself. Without the passwords, I couldn't open them.

"What the hell, Pops?" I mumbled as I looked over the files. I was frustrated as fuck as I looked over the contents of the SD cards. But something told me that whatever was on there had to be some serious shit for Pops to have it password protected and hidden in his head board. I didn't give a damn how long it took me to do it, but I planned on hacking the shit out of it. If I could figure out the code to his safe, there was no doubt in my mind I could figure this out, too.

Janaya and I stayed out of school for a week so we could grieve for Pops and get ready for his funeral. Tashai offered to come as support as well as Lamar and a lot of my friends from the

Yani

basketball team. Thankfully, Pops funeral was held on a Saturday.

The hardest part was viewing his body. I managed to keep it together until then. Seeing Pops laying in that casket like that destroyed me. It didn't even look like him. They had so much make-up on him. The longer I stared at him, the more I could see where he had taken a beaten… a severe beaten. I almost collapsed after staring at him. Meagan and Janaya held me as I cried harder and louder than I wanted to. But Pops wasn't just my father. He was my best friend and the person I trusted and looked up to more than anyone. Even though the shit came out about how Joselyn got hooked on drugs, Pops was still my father… my hero. And now he was gone.

We sat through the service and everything was going good until it came time for people to say a few words. Black people have no fucking chill.

I had only seen this bitch a few times when I was a kid, and I couldn't even remember whether or not she was at my mother's funeral. But for whatever reason, she felt the need to come to Pops' funeral and thought that was the time to disrespect his name as well as his life.

"Hi everyone. I'm Cortez's baby-momma's big sister," she spoke into the mic. She then did the trifling, hoodrat-bitch lip smacking, and I wanted to choke-slam her right then. "I only knew Cortez because my sister had kids by him but um… yeah, I like how everybody came out to show love, you know, that's a beautiful thing but um…" She stopped momentarily to smack her lips again. "People gotta learn to be real about a person in life and in death, you nah-mean. I understand Cortez might be some of y'all family and a lot of y'all friends, but don't try to make a nigga out to be more than what he was. Cortez wasn't shit. He got my sister strung out on drugs, stole her kids from her, and did a lotta other grimy shit. If it wasn't for him, my sister not only never woulda been strung out on drugs, but she never woulda OD'd. So, the way I feel, what goes around comes around and he got what the fuck he deserved. Karma…"

The loud murmur of people who were shocked and appalled at the level of disrespect could be heard throughout the church. I was already standing, intending to say a few words in memory of my father, so it didn't take much for me to get to her. As soon as she stepped away from the podium, I walked over to her, cocked my fist back, and punch that bitch dead in her fucking mouth. I had never hit a female before, and up until that moment, never would have ever put my hands on a woman. But what that bitch did was disrespectful, untimely, and out of line, but justified that punch. She'd better be glad I hit her with my left and not my right since it was encased in a cast. I saw fucking red at that moment. And had Buck not grabbed me, I would have put that bitch in the ground with Pops.

The church was in an uproar and people jumped up to see what was going on. I hit that bitch so hard she almost fell inside of Pops casket.

"Calm down, young bol'," Buck told me as I struggled against him.

"Get her the fuck out of here!" I screamed. "Get that bitch outta here or I'ma stretch her the fuck out and this'll be a double fucking funeral!"

"You're just like your fucking father! And your day is coming, too, pussy!" she shrieked through her bloody mouth. One of the church members ushered her out and I was taken to another room.

This was the angriest I had been since before Joselyn died. I thought I had my anger under control, but I couldn't focus on anything. I paced rapidly in the side room they had me in, breathing heavily.

"Davion, calm down." Buck said to me. Meagan rushed into the room and closed the door behind her.

"Fuck that!" I yelled as I continued to pace. My heavy breathing sounded more like a growl. My chest heaved in and out before I finally couldn't take it anymore and I started trashing the room, flipping tables and throwing chairs.

"Davion!" Meagan screamed. She ran over to me and grabbed me. "Please, Davion! Please! This is not what your father wanted. It's not, baby! Calm down!" She pleaded with me as she held me.

I cried like a baby in her arms. Janaya came over and hugged me as well and we hugged one another as a trio until I calmed down. After we had gotten ourselves together, Buck told us to go back to the service and he would straighten the room up.

I felt like Tupac as I made my way back to my seat at the church. The choir mistress was singing

Yani

His Eye is on the Sparrow but all eyes were on me. People whispered as they stared at me, but I didn't give a shit. And I had no problem dishing out another ass whipping if anybody dared to disrespect my father again at his funeral.

We sat in the family limo heading to the cemetery. We were all quiet, not really knowing what to say. Janaya spoke up first.

"Pops was the one who got mom turned out on drugs?" she asked. Her question exploded upon the silence in the car. Meagan and I looked at each other as Janaya looked at us.

"No," I lied.

"Then why did that lady say that? And who was she? I don't remember her."

"Because bitches always starting shit and Philly niggas are the worst. Always doing the most at the wrong times." I hissed as I looked down at my left hand. It was still throbbing a little from the punch that connected with the bitch's disrespectful mouth.

"Davion, I'm trying to be real understanding because I know you're hurt and angry over what happened with your father. But your mouth... You need to watch your mouth!" she chastised me. I shook my head and looked out the window.

"Why would that lady say that about Pops, though? Like, people don't just lie about stuff like that for nothing." Janaya pressed.

"Just drop it, Jah-Jah. People are hateful and pick the wrong times to throw shade. She's mad because things didn't work out with Pops and Joselyn. Joselyn had problems and tried to use drugs to solve them, and died. End of story." I said maliciously. It wasn't a lie, but it wasn't the whole truth either. There was no way I could tell Janaya as we were headed to bury our father, that he was the one who started Joselyn out on getting high and that's what ultimately led to her death. I could never bare the pain that truth would cause her at this time. Whoever said there's no such thing as an honest lie never told a brutal truth.

At the cemetery, Janaya, Meagan and I sat together in front of Pops casket. Janaya rested her head on my shoulder as she cried softly. She grabbed my hand and we squeezed each others, making me think back to Joselyn's funeral. The late autumn breeze blew briskly past us, shaking the last of the leaves from the branches as everyone laid roses across Pops' black and gold casket. I happened to look up and saw Tashai standing across from me on the other side of the casket. She nodded at me and I nodded back in return.

As my father's casket began to lower into the ground, a woman began singing *Precious Lord.* Janaya squeezed my hand tighter.

"I love you, Pops…" she murmured softly. I watched as his casket disappeared into the ground and looked up again. Buck was standing off to the side near Sam. He had sun glasses on with a long peat coat and a thick navy blue and gray scarf wrapped around his neck. The sunglasses hid his eyes but I could tell by looking at him that he wasn't shedding one muthafucking tear. Sam on the other hand, looked broken up. So much for my dad being his right-hand man. I stared at Buck and he stared back at me. If I didn't know any better, he had a smirk on his face. If I didn't suspect that he knew more than he led on about what happened to Pops, I was sure at that moment that he did. What's done in the dark, though…

Pops repast was being held at the church where his funeral was. But I needed to stop home first.

"Can you drop me off at the house?" I asked the driver of the limo.

"For what?" Meagan asked as she looked at me.

I hesitated. "I need to change my clothes. You know how I feel about slacks and shoes. That ain't my thing."

"Okay, but how are you going to get back to the church?" she asked.

"I can drive." I said with a charismatic smile.

"With what license?"

I sucked my teeth. "Come on, Meagan. You let me drive when we had to get Jah-Jah from school. But if it's a problem, I'll just catch the bus."

Meagan looked at me for a moment as though she was thinking. Her face lightened up as she sighed, giving in. "Fine." She tossed me the keys after digging them out of her purse. "Don't jack up my car, Davion. I mean it. And don't get used to driving, either. As soon as things calm down and your hand is better, get your license because after

Yani

today, that's the only way you're going to be pushing my whip."

I grinned eagerly as I tucked the keys in my coat pocket. The limo dropped me off and I went into the house. I immediately went over to the safe. Thankfully, the code hadn't been changed. All of the money as well as Pops gun was in there. I took everything out and put it inside of a bag. I was betting Meagan didn't know about the safe.

I went out back to our shed and used a couple of crates to stand on so I could reach the top of the shed. From my bedroom, I always suspected the pipe next to it could be moved and sure enough, I was able to pull it partially from the wall. I made sure no one was watching and stuffed the money and the gun inside of the pipe before readjusting it. I then jumped down and went back in the house.

I went up to Meagan and Pops' room and moved the headboard. Imagine my surprise when I saw that everything that had been hidden in there was gone. The hard drives, the SD cards and the money were all gone. I put the headboard back and stood in the middle of the room feeling dumb founded. If Meagan knew about what was hidden in the headboard but didn't know about the safe, where the fuck did she put what was in there? Better yet, why did she move it and even more importantly, who the fuck did she give it to? I had a thought and rushed to my bedroom. I snatched my MacBook from off of the bed and checked the side of it. I closed my eyes and let out a sigh of relief. The SD card was still in there. I took it out and snatched the tape from off of my desk before partially sliding under my bed. I used the tape to attach the SD card to the inner part of my bed beam. Now I was more determined than ever to figure out what was on there.

I changed out of the dress clothes that I wore to Pops' funeral and threw on a pair of True Religion jeans with a long-sleeved Polo shirt and a pair of Jordans. Since I had Meagan's car, I left my coat home and grabbed my hoody instead.

I managed to squeeze into a parking spot not too far from the church and went inside where everyone was. The smell of piping hot, fried chicken with greens, baked macaroni and cheese, seafood and potato salad, sweet Hawaiian rolls and loads of other delicious eats filled the air and made my stomach growl. Folks were seated around a

Yani

large wooden table with plates in front of them while others were either seated in various chairs with plates in their laps or standing near a wall, holding their plates and feeding their faces. I knew the smell of Ms. Aretha's food anywhere, long as I had been eating at her house. Buck, Sam and Meagan were still in their little group, eating food and talking. The site of them linked up like that rubbed me the wrong way. A part of me tried to tell myself that maybe they were trying to piece together what happened to Pops. But another part of me was suspicious of them and I couldn't shake that feeling.

I was about to fix myself a plate when I peeped Janaya sitting close to Lamar. She picked at a piece of chicken on her plate as she talked to him. I hadn't seen Tashai and wondered if she'd gone back home after the burial.

After loading up my plate with Ms. Aretha's delicious eats, I snagged a chair that someone had gotten up from and dragged it over to where Lamar and Janaya were sitting.

"What's up, y'all?" I spoke as I purposely sat between them. Janaya shook her head at me as she continued to pick at her chicken.

"'Sup, Dah-Dah? I was just asking Janaya where you were." Lamar spoke back casually as though nothing was going on.

"I stopped past the house to change my clothes. You know I don't bang with that suit and tie shit. I ain't Justin Timberlake." We chuckled together. Janaya still remained quiet.

"Yeah, I saw you pushing Meagan's whip the other day," Lamar said with a smirk. I didn't respond either way, choosing instead to eat my food as I watched Buck, Sam and Meagan. "What was up with the chick at the funeral, yo? That shit was foul, man."

"Yeah, that's why I popped that bitch in her fucking mouth," I hissed.

"Who was she?" Lamar asked.

"One of Joselyn's sisters. My thing is, if you knew your sister was on drugs, why the fuck you ain't try to help her get off that shit? Why you ain't step in to help with us when shit was all fucked up in the house? Don't show up talking reckless at my dad's funeral, talking like y'all all broken up over what happened with Joselyn, trying to throw blame, when you ain't even try to fucking help her." I was hot. Just thinking about how that bitch disrespected at Pops' service made me want to find her and stomp her fucking mouth.

"I feel you, homie. And I probably would've done the same shit. Real rap," Lamar replied. I finished my food and noticed that Sam and Buck seemed to be in a bit of a heated discussion, but on the low. I don't know what was being said, but whatever it was, Sam didn't like that shit at all. Meagan appeared to be trying to reason with Sam but he snatched away from her and walked out of the room shaking his head. What the hell was going on with them, is what I was wondering?

Being around everybody, sharing stories while we laughed and reminisced helped ease the pain we were all feeling from Pops' absence. But it was like putting a band aid over a knife wound that had been cut too deeply. Once the people began to leave and the laughter and chatter died down, we were forced to deal with the harsh reality that Pops was gone and was never coming back.

During the ride home, Janaya rested her head on my shoulder for comfort. I couldn't stop staring at Meagan. There was so much running through my mind like where the fuck was the money and SD cards that Pops had in the headboard and what was the beef about between her Sam and Buck. I decided to wait before I started to question her. That was the beauty about the truth, it always revealed itself eventually.

After we got home, Meagan said she was going to take a nap and Janaya went up to her room and closed her door. That was pretty much her routine ever since we found out that Pops had been killed. I planned to talk to her to make sure I helped her through this.

I walked through the house, trying to force myself to get used to the silence. I wished to God that Pops would walk through the door with his usual energetic self and talk to me, crack jokes, or hit me with some words of wisdom. I looked at the family photos that we had on top of a table in the dining room before I picked up the one of Pops. He was wearing a red Polo shirt with white stripes and a pair of cargo shorts with a pair of Jordans. He was holding a Heineken in one hand and leaned on his truck looking off to the side with a grin on his face as though someone had cracked a super funny joke. I missed his laugh. His laugh made us all laugh. I had to get out of that house at that moment. I felt like I was suffocating and the sadness from this recent loss was consuming me. I immediately texted Tashai.

"What's up, Shorty? You busy?" I said in the text.

A few minutes later, she texted back. *"No I was laying across the bed reading a book. My mom was called in to work so I'm in the house by myself again."* She put a sad emoji face on the end.

I still had Meagan's keys so I grabbed my coat and headed over to the front door. *"I'm on my way."* I texted her as I shut and locked the door behind me. I jumped in Meagan's car and headed over to Tashai's house. I could hear her playing the piano from the porch and I listened for a moment. She was playing *"Halo"* by Beyonce and it actually sounded like the album. After listening for a moment, I rang the doorbell.

"Hey," Tashai said with a smile after opening the door for me. I wrapped my arms around her and hugged her tightly after she opened the door wider for me to come in.

"What'chu getting ready for a talent show or something?" I asked her as I sat near the piano.

"Oh… no I just wanted to learn something new and was watching some YouTube videos. I saw this Black guy playing this and it sounded so dope so I figured I would try, too." Tashai said as she sat at the piano.

"How long you been working on it?" I asked her as I tapped a few of the keys.

"Oh, I just started when I came from your dad's burial."

I looked at her with my eyebrows raised. "Seriously? Yo, Shorty you got a gift, man. Straight up. You gotta do something with that. Don't let that go to waste."

She sighed and stared at the piano for a moment. "I've been hearing that a lot. My mom is finally going to send me to music school so I can learn how to read music because I want to apply to Juilliard in New York for college. So, I really gotta be on my grind because it's kids from all over that can play Beethoven like they got twenty fingers applying there." We both burst out laughing.

"You funny as shit for that one. Can you sing and play at the same time?" I asked her.

Yani

Tashai smiled bashfully. "Yeah, but I don't like to, though."

"Come on, let me hear you. It's just you and me. Ain't nobody gonna know." I urged her as I playfully elbowed her. She blushed and then stared at the piano for a moment as though she were thinking. She then began playing *"If I Ain't Got You"* by Alicia Keys. I was shocked by her voice when she began singing. I thought it was going to have that bubbly-pop music sound to it. But it was sultry and bluesy sounding. The way her voice rifted over a few of the notes and the strength in her voice at the high parts sent chills down my spine. When she finished, she waited a moment before glancing at me.

"I messed up a couple times," she said quietly before she closed the piano.

"I didn't notice. That shit was mad dope, yo. Damn…" was all I could say as I shook my head. She reached for my cast and gently rubbed it.

"What's going to happen with USC and the rest of the season?" she asked me.

"I thought I was going to be out for the rest of the season but only six to eight weeks, which is still too long. But at least I'll get to play in the playoffs. My hand should be cool by late January, early February." I told her She fell silent as I began to play with her fingers. She definitely had piano hands with long slender fingers. Her nails were neatly manicured but she was wearing her real nails instead of the fake ones chicks were always getting from the nail salon. I intertwined our fingers together as I thought about Pops. He had only met her once but I could tell he liked her a lot. Thinking of all of the things he was going to miss out on with me and Janaya brought the sorrow back. I squeezed Tashai's hand as a way to give me strength. I didn't want to grieve anymore and I hated the way the pain crept up on me at random times. Tashai squeezed my hand back as though she understood and kissed me on my forehead.

"It's okay," she told me softly.

I shook my head as I tried hard not to let the tears fall. It wasn't okay and it wasn't going to be okay any time soon.

I needed something that would take my mind off losing my father and Joselyn. I needed something that would make the pain go away, even if it was only temporarily. I pulled Tashai closer so

Yani

I could kiss her. The void within could only be filled by her and I needed her to fill it for me. I slid my hand up the back of her shirt and unclipped her bra before gently grabbing her breasts and squeezing them. She breathed deeply against my mouth before breaking our kiss. I could see a hint of fear in her eyes, more than likely from what had been done to her. I didn't think words would comfort her or assure her that I would never hurt her like she had been hurt before.

Tashai closed her eyes appearing as though she was thinking or deciding what choice to make. I needed her to choose me at that moment. She backed away from me and my heart sank, thinking that I wasn't her choice.

"Come on…" she said softly before walking over to her stair case. I stood up and followed behind her.

Her room was smaller than mine, but neat and clean with a full-sized bed covered with a royal blue flower-patterned comforter set. The first thing I noticed was that her mirror was covered with a black sheet. Paul Laurence Dunbar's poem flashed through my mind. *We Wear the Mask*. I assumed Tashai didn't have a mask and the sheet over the mirror was her way of shielding herself from seeing something within herself that only her reflection would show.

Before Tashai, I had been with four other girls. Nothing intimate. Just a straight hit and roll. But it was different with Tashai. I took my time with her and explored her, wanting to learn what her likes and dislikes were. Being with her showed me the difference between fucking and making love.

Tashai shook underneath me when we were done, and clung to me. After she'd calmed down a bit, I pulled away from her so I could flush the condom down the toilet. On my way back to her room, I noticed a few envelopes on a small table in the hallway. I stopped in mid-step. One of the envelopes sticking halfway out caught my attention. I picked it up and stared at it.

"Babe?" I called out to her.

"Yes?" she answered back.

"What's *Vivint?*" I asked.

"Oh, that's a security system my mom got after my dad was killed. It comes with cameras and stuff. It's her way of keeping an eye on the house and me to make sure everything is cool. Why?"

I put the envelope back the way I found it as my mind began racing. I had a straight up "Oh shit" moment. I came back in the room and sat on the side of the bed so I could get dressed.

"Explain it," I said to her as I pulled my tank top over my head.

"Oh, don't worry. There aren't any cameras in my room if that's what you're worried about." Tashai assured me.

"Nah, I'm not thinking about that. But if it's a camera in your living room, would your mom have been able to see us come up to your room?" I asked as I looked at her. Tashai winced as she thought of what I said and then hung her head.

"I didn't even think of that…" she said as she shook her head. "But I doubt my mom really watches the footage anyways. We more so use it to see who's at the door when they ring the doorbell and if we're away for like a weekend or longer, my mom can check the house to make sure nobody is in here. She can even talk to people from her phone when they ring the doorbell as though she is here, but be all the way in Jersey at work, and they don't even know it," she giggled.

"Wait…you have cameras outside of your house?" I asked her.

"Yeah. Right above the doorbell. There's another in the corner of the window and one above the door. There's two in the living room on different sides, one in the dining room, one in the kitchen and two out back. There's also two in the hallway. My mom was on some other time when she got it. Made me feel like I was being watched."

I continued to get dressed as I listened to Tashai. I thought back to the SD cards that were in the headboard and the files on the one card that I'd swiped. Pops had cameras in the house. But why?

"You good?" Tashai asked me as she studied my face.

I shook my head. "I think we have the same thing at our house but I never noticed any cameras. So, if I wanted to look at the footage, how would I if it's not connected to my phone?

"There's SD Cards with video footage on them. My mom uses a combination of my birthday with hers for the password."

Yani

"Is it case sensitive or does it have to have special characters?" I asked as I put my sneakers on.

"Yup. Case sensitive and special characters, and it has to be at least seven characters long."

"What if I don't know the password or forgot it? How do I get it again? Or can I reset it?"

"Yeah, just go to the website. If you know the email address and telephone number the account was started with, you can either have them send the password to the email address or send you a text message."

"Text me the link. I gotta run back home. I can't explain now, but we're gonna talk tonight, alright." I said to her as I stood up. Tashai looked up at me and nodded her head. I knelt in front of her and grabbed her chin before kissing her. I was falling hard for this girl and wanted to tell her, but something held me back. Instead I kissed her again and then left her room.

I couldn't wait to get back home. Something told me that if I was able to get access to whatever was on that SD card, I was going to find out some big shit. When I got to the house, I paid more attention to the outside of it, looking upward. I noticed the cameras on the outside which blended in really well with the bricks. I then walked over to the side of the house and noticed the camera up there as well as the two in the back. It then dawned on me that there could possibly be footage of who broke into the house.

I walked back around front and used my key to get in. I was startled when I saw Buck sitting at the counter talking to Meagan. The muthafucka was posted up like he fucking lived there. Meagan looked nervous.

"Where the hell were you?" Meagan asked me.

"With my girl," I said flatly as I walked over to the steps.

"Boy, give me my damn keys. I told you, you wasn't driving my damn car without a license. Stop trying me, Davion." Meagan warned.

I stared at her for a moment feeling ice in my veins. I then glanced at Buck. This fuck nigga seemed like a snake to me. If I could see that at sixteen, what the fuck took Pops so long to peep this nigga wasn't real.

I wasn't in the mood to be arguing with her, so I reached in my pocket, grabbed her keys and politely put them in her hand without saying anything.

"The next time you wanna lay up with your little girlfriend, get on the damn bus. And the least you could've done was shower before you came back here. Coming in here smelling like pussy." Meagan hissed as she went back to the counter to sit with Buck.

"Your day coming, bitch." I mumbled as I went upstairs.

"You gon' have a problem with that little nigga, watch." I heard Buck say as I reached the top of the landing.

I went in my room and closed and locked my bedroom door, immediately pulling my MacBook out and taking the SD card that was taped to my bed's beams. After putting the SD card inside, I saw my phone flash with a text message from Tashai. She sent me the link as asked. I typed it in the web browser as my heart thudded in my chest, nervous about what I might come across. I didn't have Pops' phone so it was no point in having them send the password reset information that way. I knew Pops' email address and password, so I had them send it there. After a few seconds, the email popped up. For some reason, something told me to copy the info from the email and then delete the email itself. Once I did, I followed the steps to get access to the SD Card. I actually didn't need the SD Card. All of the video footage was in Pops' account and available for me to see. I noticed there was one with that day's date on it. I clicked on it and saw that it was of Buck and Meagan.

"Oh shit…" I mumbled. They were being recorded at that very moment. I hesitated on clicking on the footage, scared of what I might see or hear. After a moment's pause, I finally clicked the video and lowered the volume so I could see what the fuck they were up to and why this nigga was showing his face so much even with Pops being gone.

"Tez is out, now," Buck was saying as he sat at the kitchen counter. "So, Constantine is on some chill shit and ready to finish doing business. And he got some serious weight he's ready to start moving with me as the main distributor. I just need you to keep shit legit with the store and your shop."

"Yeah, but I'm not going to keep sticking my neck out, putting all this skin in this shit but ain't getting hit off with at least two-fifty. Fuck that. I did my part and I'm done with this rah-rah shit."

"I got you, Meg. Trust me. We about to take this shit to a whole 'nother level, feel me. Fuck that rebel-take over shit. We 'bouta own these streets. Philly gon' be ours. Everybody gon' cop from us and if not…" Buck shrugged. "After what happened to Tez, you think they gon' try to flex on us now?"

Meagan didn't respond. She instead took a sip from a wine glass. I watched in fury as Buck stood up and walked behind Meagan. They both looked to the top of the stairs as though they were making sure no one was coming. Buck then grabbed Meagan by her hair and made her bend over the counter. The smirk on her face made me want to body that bitch. She was still dressed in the skirt suit she wore to Pops' funeral. Buck hiked her skirt up and ripped her stockings off before unzipping his pants and pulling them down. Meagan arched her back before reaching behind her to grab on Buck so she could slide him inside of her. And right there in my Pops' kitchen, looking like they had done this numerous times before, I watched as Buck bussed her ass. That hoe-bag-ass bitch was fucking my

Pops' right hand man in the kitchen that he paid for not even a day after his body was in the ground.

After Buck nutted inside of her, he fixed his clothes and Meagan threw her torn stockings in the trash quickly. She straightened out her clothes and then dipped to the refrigerator as Buck sat casually at the counter like they hadn't just finished fucking. I saw Janaya emerge from the dining room and then I exited out of the footage.

That fucking snake-bitch! She got the balls to be fucking his mans in our house. No, fuck that- MY HOUSE!! She been fucking this nigga behind Pops' back and either helped set him up or knew he was being set up so Buck's bitch-ass could slide into a better position of power! Nah, I was hot. I wanted to fly down those muthafucking steps and put both their asses to sleep.

"Never let your left hand know what your right hand is doing," I heard Pops voice in my head as though he was warning me to chill like he had done many times when I was younger and ran into a problem. Revenge is best served when the muthafucka doesn't see it coming. Those were also words I heard him use before. I wondered at that moment

if Pops knew and had a plan in works to deal with them.

My phone rang and I saw it was Tashai. I didn't want her to feel like I smutted her so I answered even though my mind was everywhere and I was pissed.

"Yo babe," I answered the phone as I sat back on my bed.

"Hey, did you get the link?" Tashai asked.

"Yeah, I got it. Thanks." I replied as I still worked on calming down. I then had an idea to reach out to Sam after remembering how he didn't appear to look so pleased at my father's repast.

"Is everything okay?" I heard Tashai ask me.

"Nah, Shorty. It's not. We're good though. So, I don't want you to think that something is wrong with us. It's just a lot of shit going on that I'm trying to wrap my head around and it's fucking with me right now." I explained.

"Oh… do you want to talk about it?" she offered.

I blew out air as I shook my head. "Not yet because like I said, I still haven't wrapped my head around this shit. But when I get it together, you know I'ma come to you, alright?" I assured her.

"Okay."

"I care about you a lot, Tashai. I want you to know that. I need to handle some shit right quick, but I'ma holla at you tonight before I go to bed, alright?"

"Okay… Davion," she called to me before I disconnected the call.

"What's up?"

"If you saw something in that footage that could help with your dad's murder, you should let the cops know," she told me. "Because I care about you, too and I don't think I could handle it if anything happened to you, too."

"Ain't nothing gonna happen to me, Shorty. I promise. But I got you, alright?"

"Okay. Call me later," she said softly.

"I will." I disconnected the call and went downstairs. It took every ounce of self-control to keep me from knocking Buck the fuck out when I saw he had his arm around Janaya as though he was comforting her.

"Jah-Jah, come take a walk with me." I said to my sister.

"Where y'all going?" Meagan asked.

Yani

I hesitated for a moment. "To get something to eat," I lied.

"All that food from earlier," Meagan frowned. "Seriously."

"Only thing I ate was what Ms. Aretha cooked. I ain't trust that other stuff. Niggas ain't real so I can't be eating everybody's cooking, dig me?" I looked at Buck for a second and then looked back at Meagan.

Meagan looked at her watch. "It's almost 8 o'clock. Don't stay out too late."

"Whatever," I mumbled as I walked towards the front door. I snatched my coat from the closet and Janaya grabbed hers with a puzzled expression on her face. When we got outside Janaya stuffed her hands in her pockets.

"Yo, I don't want you nowhere near Buck, you hear me?"

Janaya frowned. "Seriously Davion, Buck is like our uncle. He was only trying to cheer me up, it ain't like that. Ill, that's nasty."

"I ain't talking on that type time, Jah-Jah." I said sternly.

Janaya fell silent for a moment. "Okay… but again, Buck is like our uncle. Why…?"

I cut her off, raising my voice. "That nigga ain't like no uncle to us, alright? Stay the fuck away from him. I mean that shit. That nigga a fucking snake. I don't want you nowhere 'round him. Straight up."

"Davion, why are you cursing at me? I didn't do nothing!" Janaya argued, sounding as though she was close to tears. "Buck's been Pops' best friend since they were your age. If he was a snake, don't you think Pops' would've cut him off already?"

I blew out air again. "Sorry for snapping on you. But you gotta trust me on this, okay. Something is up with that nigga. I can't put my finger on it, but something is really up with that nigga. I feel that shit in my gut and Pops always told us that going against your gut is like going against the grain; you don't do it. So, don't ask me any questions, just stay away from that nigga, alright?"

I'd hoped that Janaya didn't ask me anymore questions or try to get me to go deeper into why I didn't want her around Buck's bitch-ass. Thankfully she didn't.

"Where we going to eat?" she asked instead.

Yani

"Nowhere. I just said that because I ain't feel like explaining shit to Meagan."

"You got beef with Meagan, too?"

I hesitated, definitely knowing for sure that I had no business telling Janaya what I knew about Meagan. I hated lying to my sis. "Nah… she cool. I'm just fucked up behind everything that's happened to us. Like, this shit is fucked up on so many levels."

"What if Meagan doesn't want us? Where will we go?" Janaya asked as she looked up at me.

I hadn't even thought of the possibility of Meagan kicking us to the curb. "I don't think she would do that. She practically helped raise us," I said in a low voice. We walked on in silence, with the cold air, chilling us. My mind was on so many things as I tried to figure out what my next move should be and what I should do about Meagan and Buck that the cold night air didn't faze me.

"Can we go back home?" Janaya asked, interrupting my thoughts. "It's too cold to be walking around out here for nothing."

"Yeah, you right." I agreed as we turned towards home.

Hoop Dreams Deflated

When we got back in the house, Buck was gone and Meagan had gone upstairs to her room. Janaya went up to her room and closed her door. That had become a norm for her since Pops was killed. I had other things on my mind though. My first line of business was dealing with Meagan. Somehow, some way, that bitch had to go...

3rd Quarter

*W*eeks had gone by with me having to put on a

performance to suggest that I had no clue what the fuck Meagan and Buck were up to. During Christmas, I put on a performance that should have granted me a fucking Academy Award, pretending that I was grateful to have Meagan in our lives and that Buck was a stand-up dude for checking in on us from time to time to make sure we were cool.

It turned out that Meagan was truly pregnant, and though she paraded around publicly that Pops was the father of that baby, something deep down inside told me that that was really Buck's baby. That bitch wasn't slick and neither was he. But I played cool like everything was all good.

It killed me that I couldn't catch up to Sam. He hadn't come around since Pops' funeral and I couldn't get his number out of Meagan's phone. I did realize that Meagan didn't know Pops had the Vivint cameras in the house. It took me a while to figure out where they were but I was able to locate all of them. I spent a lot of time catching up on footage, which was painful at times, seeing Pops move throughout the house and seeing all the times we shared as a family, but knowing that we would never have times like that again. I made sure I stayed focused on the task at hand, which was finding out who the fuck Constantine was as well as who broke into the house.

Tashai and I spent a lot of time together. Unfortunately, her mother did happen to check the footage and saw when we went up to her room. I didn't know that up until that day, Tashai was a virgin, minus the incident with her uncle. Knowing that her little girl had had sex in her home while she was at work set her off and I was banned from their house until she had the opportunity to meet me. She grilled the shit out of me when I came to the house for dinner. But after I told her what my intentions were for myself as well as for Tashai, and she knew that I could possibly still head to college a year early on a basketball scholarship, she lightened up on me.

Yani

The coach was able to work some things out with the counselor as well as the administration at USC where I could still graduate early, but I would have to take a summer course to ensure I had the credits I needed to officially get my diploma and then move on to USC. Because we were up against the clock, I was scheduled immediately for a weekend tour of the campus. I was in my bedroom packing when Janaya tapped on my door.

"What's up, Jah?" I asked as I was folding a shirt.

"I wish I could come with you," Janaya mumbled.

"Well, you can always come visit sometimes," I suggested. Since Janaya was old enough to crawl, we had been inseparable.

"Yeah right," she snorted. "You know Megan ain't gonna let me fly out to California to stay with you for a weekend or anything else. And with the funny way she been acting in here since Pops died, I don't want to be in here with her by myself."

"Acting funny like what?" I asked with my back to her. I never told her about the cameras that were in the house or that Megan was a sneaky-ass bitch that was fucking Pops' right hand man, was more than likely pregnant by him and may have played a part in setting him up to be killed.

Janaya shrugged. "I dunno. It's kinda hard to explain. It's just going to suck here without you. At least if Pops was still here…" she trailed off and I knew she was trying not to cry.

I sighed as I put my last shirt in my suitcase. "Come here, Jah-Jah." I sat on the bed and she sat next to me. She rested her head on my shoulder for comfort and I put my arm around her. I wasn't really sure what to say to her to comfort her. "I miss Pops, too." I said after we shared a moment of silence. Her cell-phone vibrated with a text and she looked at it discreetly.

"I'll be back," she said in a low voice as she left the room. I was curious about who that was texting her, but I promised I wouldn't be hawking and stalking over her in creep mode, as she put it. I trusted that if she needed to talk to me about a boy, she would be comfortable enough to come to me. But if I find out a nigga is trying to dog my little sister, he's gonna catch these hands like no other.

I got up from my bed and went downstairs to grab a snack and something to drink. I heard

Yani

Meagan on the phone talking to someone, so I waited at the bottom of the steps to listen in for a moment.

"You haven't shown your face around here since Tez's funeral and now you wanna call to see how everybody is doing. Sounds more like you wanna make sure we're all on the same page about the agreement… I'm just sayin', Sam… I'm good on this end and the kids are good, too… Yeah okay… You do the same…"

The call ended and I came the rest of the way down the stairs, pretending as though I didn't hear anything.

"What's good, Meagan?" I spoke blandly as I headed over to the refrigerator.

"Nothing much. You finished packing?" she asked in return.

"Yeah, I just put the last of my stuff in my suitcase and made sure my plane ticket and everything else is in my bag." I assured her.

"Good, good, good," she said in return as she leaned into the counter. She looked worried, or like she was under a lot of stress. Maybe the guilt was getting to her.

I fixed myself a bowl of ice-cream and noticed she had the new Samsung Note 5. I had been wanting to get in contact with Sam for a while ever since I saw the way he stormed out of Pop's repass, but I never got a chance to since he stopped coming around. I stuck a spoonful of ice-cream in my mouth as I eyed her phone.

"That's the new Samsung jawn?" I asked.

Meagan looked at her phone and then slid it over to me. "Yeah. I got it earlier today because my Note 4 was acting nutty. It was time for an upgrade anyway."

"This jawn look tough. Can I see it?" I asked. Not thinking much about it, she unlocked her phone and gave it to me. I pretended to geek over her phone as I searched through it for Sam's number. I found him in her contacts and sent his number to my phone as a text message and then deleted it. I geeked over it a little longer before I gave it back to her.

"That jawn is fire. But I'm still team iPhone," I laughed before I headed upstairs with my bowl of ice-cream.

Yani

After closing the door behind me, I quickly saved Sam's number to my phone. I wanted to text him right then but fear of what he might tell me held me back. I figured it would be best if I waited until after my trip to contact him.

The next morning,, I woke up, showered and got dressed for my flight to USC. Janaya rode with us and gave me a huge hug before I went to board my flight. Meagan's fake ass gave me a hug as well.

Touring the campus renewed my vision for my future as an NBA basketball star. After seeing how huge the campus was and how the gym was filled with state of the art equipment, I became even more excited about attending that college.

During the flight back home, I couldn't stop obsessing over my pending future at USC. I put my Beats headphones on and zoned out as I fantasized about playing in an NCAA championship and being the talk of every sports outlet. I felt it in every part of my body that I was on my way to doing big things. My only wish was that Pops and Joselyn could physically be there to see me accomplish those things.

After getting off the flight, I got a text message from Meagan letting me know that she wasn't able to get me from the airport because she had to work at the salon late, but that she ordered me an Uber. Gee, how thoughtful.

It was fucking freezing outside, which was a twist since I had just come back from sunny California where it was 80 degrees, sunshine, palm trees, and chicks in bikinis. Here in Philly, it was every bit of two degrees with a breeze, and the only thing half-naked were trees. I chuckled to myself as I thought *"Bars."*

I went through my phone and saw Sam's number. I decided to swallow my fear and sent him a text message.

"Yo Unc, this Davion. I need to talk to you. It's important."

I figured he was busy and wouldn't get back to me until later on that evening. He shocked the hell out of me when he hit me right back.

"Yo youngin'. I been wanting to get at you but Meagan been blocking. What's on your mind?"

We texted back in forth for a bit with me trying to fill Sam out to see what position he was in with Buck and Meagan. He was very up front about everything and told me he knew months before

Yani

Pops was killed that something was going on between Buck and Meagan. He believed Meagan let Buck get in her head and manipulate her into setting Pops up so that Buck could move into a position of power, being Constantine's main distributor for the tristate area.

"So, Constantine wasn't after Pops. Buck was? Did Pops know this?" I asked Sam.

"Not until it was too late. When I realized what Meagan and Buck were up to, I tried to put a bug in his ear. I had been warning him for a while that Buck was the one putting the heat to him, but he didn't want to believe his right-hand man was grimy like that. It was enough in the game for all of us to eat but he was on some take over shit."

It took me a minute to respond to Sam. A part of me blamed him for not trying harder to show Pops what was up. But I remembered how stubborn my father was, and that, eventually, was his downfall.

I guess the guilt was eating away at Sam even more when I didn't respond right away because he texted me again.

"Davion, I'm sorry I didn't do more to look out for your Pops. I never expected them to go this far. I thought they were just going to convince him to retire and have Constantine

move Buck into your Pops position. But I was wrong. And I'm sorry."

"It's cool, Unc. A man is going to do his own thing no matter what you tell him. Thanks for being real with me."

"No prob, nephew."

I stared at my phone for a while re-reading the conversation between me and Sam as the Uber driver weaved in and out of traffic to get me home. He dropped some serious gems on me. I swear niggas in Philly are the worst. They'll skin and grin in your face, pop bottles with you and pretend to celebrate your success, all the while them snake-ass niggas either plotting on your downfall or scheming on how to take your place. It's always the ones closest to you that fucks you over.

I had my tablet with me and decided to look at footage from the day Pops disappeared. Pops was upstairs in the shower and Meagan was on the phone with Buck. I listened as she assured Buck that Pops would be at the spot for them to meet up with him. She then called upstairs for him.

"Babe!" she hollered from at the bottom of the steps. "I need you to head over to Limekiln Pike near Medary to meet with the broker for that building so we can open another store."

"I was supposed to handle inventory today. I thought you said the meeting was tomorrow?" Pops asked as he came half-way down the stairs.

"The guy just called and said he has to go out of town tomorrow and could only do it today and I have appointments at the salon," Meagan lied.

"Alright, I'll take care of it." Pops said to her. After he finished getting dressed, he came down the stairs and gave Meagan a hug and a kiss before telling her that he loved her and would be home for dinner. She smiled lovingly and watched him as he left. She then made a phone call.

"He's on his way. Don't forget what we agreed on. I want this done with as of today."

I sat back with my mouth gaped open. As far as I was concerned, Meagan had just given the order to kill my father. I was hot in the back of that Uber car. The fury that was rising inside of me almost felt uncontrollably. I kept hearing my father telling me a man is only as weak as his ability to control his emotions. Never let your left hand know what your right hand is doing. I took deep breaths trying to adhere to my father's warning, but the pain of seeing footage of Pops in the house, hearing Meagan give the order to kill him, and knowing he would never be there with us again because of her and Buck was too much. But now I knew. The only question that remained was, what was I going to do next?

The Uber dropped me off and was kind enough to wait to make sure I got in the house before he drove off. Janaya was lounging on the couch talking on her cell-phone when I walked in. The moment she saw me, she abruptly ended the conversation and sat her phone to the side.

"Hey Davion!" she perked, excited to see me. "I thought you weren't going to be back until later."

"Nah, my flight landed early and Meagan had an Uber come pick me up. Is she here?"

"No, she's still at the shop. She already cooked though, if you're hungry."

"Nah, I'm good," I told her as I headed up to my room. I closed and locked my bedroom door as I felt an eerie calm wash over me. I tossed my suitcase and duffle bag onto the floor and leaned onto my window sill as I looked out into the darkness. I lift my window and partially climbed out so I could reach the pipe where I hid Pops' money and his gun. I never bothered to count the money or see what else was with it since I just slid everything into a bag. I got what I wanted and put everything else back in its' hiding spot.

"Where are you going?" Janaya asked as I clamored down the steps.

"Nowhere. I'll be back," I said blandly as I left out of the house and closed the door behind myself before she could say anything else. I pulled my hoody up over my head as I made my way over to the salon. I knew it was closing time so I decided to come through the back way. I was expecting to have to climb through a window or something but was pleasantly surprised when I saw Meagan had the backdoor opened so she could sit the trash outside. I slipped inside and into the bathroom, peeking out as I watched her drag a big green trash bag out to the alley. She then went over to her office to take care of paper work.

I reached down in my pocket and felt the chrome handle of the 9mm. Every nerve in my body shook as I curled my hand around it. I began to have second thoughts about what I was going to do, but I knew there was no turning back now. I closed my eyes and took a deep breath. Yes, there was definitely no turning back now.

My foot steps were quiet and stealth as I made my way to her office. I peeked inside and saw that her back was to me which made this even easier. I stepped closer to her as my heart thudded in my chest. I prayed she didn't turn around before I got close enough to her, though the idea of shooting her in the face had merit. She was so engrossed in her work that she didn't even realize what was waiting for her.

I pulled the gun from my pocket slowly and pointed it at the back of her head. She froze when she heard me chamber a round.

"If you're here to rob me, please just…"

"Bitch, I don't want yo' muthafuckin' money," I seethed through clenched teeth.

Meagan hesitated for a moment as it took time for it to register that it was me behind her. "Davion…? What the hell…?"

"Shut up! Shut up, you lying, cheating snake-ass bitch!" I hissed as I pushed the back of her head with the muzzle of the gun.

Yani

"Okay… okay. Just tell me what's wrong, Davion? Talk to me and we can work this out."

"Ain't shit to talk about. I know everything. I know you ordered Buck to kill Pops. I know you've been fucking that nigga for months. Months! My father gave ya hoe-ass everything and you fucking set him up!"

Meagan breathed deeply and I could hear where she was crying. "It's not as cut and dry as you think, Davion. It's more to this than you know…" she quickly tried to explain.

"No! No, I don't wanna fucking hear it. You might as well had pulled the trigger and dumped his body yourself. You're every bit as responsible as the niggas who actually did it."

"So that's it? You're a man now? If you pull that trigger, you're no better than us! It won't take the pain away and it's not what your father would want." Meagan said calmly as she sniffed back her tears.

I held the gun with both of my hands as I aimed it at the back of her head, trembling. Tears stung my eyes and no matter how hard I tried to blink them back, they managed to break through and fall anyway.

"What about my baby, Davion? If you kill me, you'll be killing your brother or sister. Is that what you want? It's your father's baby!" Meagan pleaded with me as she tried to appeal to my conscience.

It was her last comment that helped with my final decision. "That ain't my father's baby, bitch," I seethed. I squeezed the trigger and the kick back from the gun caused me to stumble a few steps back before falling to the floor. I thought I missed until I heard the dripping sound that Meagan's blood was making as it hit the floor. I leaned forward and felt the warmth from her blood on my face and neck that came from the blow back of the shot. She was slumped over her desk as the contents of her head spilled out. Dead… I killed her.

Panic washed over me. I scrambled to my feet and looked around trying to figure out what I should do next. I trashed her office and then went into her safe and took the money out, grateful for the gloves that I had on which would keep my finger prints from being all over the place. I then grabbed the security footage, relieved that she didn't have Vivint so I didn't have to worry about hacking her footage. She had a regular old security camera and CD that held what was recorded. I left back out of the back door and made my way back home.

I was grateful when I got in the house and saw that Janaya had gone up to her room. I went to my own and locked my bedroom door. I grabbed a wife beater and a pair of ball shorts to change into before I put the gun and money I took from Meagan's office in my hiding spot and then went to the bathroom to take my shower. I knew eventually I would have to ditch that gun and the clothes.

The hot, steamy shower water rained down on me as I couldn't help but to think about what I had just done. I killed someone… The echo from the gunshot played again and again in my head. And no matter how hard I scrubbed my face, I could still feel her blood on my skin.

After thoroughly scrubbing my body, I got out of the shower and filled the sink with hot water and bleach. I then soaked my hands in the water for a little over five minutes to make sure there was no gun powder on my hands or wrists. I remembered reading somewhere about that being the best way to get the residue off of you without leaving a trace.

I knew I needed an alibi, but didn't want to involve Janaya. I didn't have much of a choice, though. She was my ride or die and I knew she would cover for me better than anyone else.

I knocked on her bedroom door and waited.

"Huh?" Janaya answered.

"Can I come in?" I asked from the other side of the door.

"I'll call you right back," I heard her say. "You can come in."

I opened her door and then closed it behind me so I could lean on it. I couldn't look at Janaya, so I looked at the floor. The silence was awkward and unbearable.

"What's up, Davion? You good?" Janaya asked me.

I sighed before I looked at her. "If anybody asks, I was here the whole night. I never left when I came in from the airport, you got it?"

Janaya detected the seriousness in my voice but that didn't stop her from firing questions my way. "Why would anyone ask where you were tonight? Where did you go, and what's going on

Yani

with you? You've been acting funny ever since you came back from USC."

"All you need to know is I came in a little after 7:30. If you need help remembering that just make sure you associate it with the time you got off the phone earlier. We watched Fast Five, ate dinner and then you sat on the phone while I was in my room watching TV, alright?"

"Davion…?" she began to question.

I interrupted her with my hand up while raising my voice. "Alright?!"

"Okay…" Janaya said softly. She waited a moment before speaking again. "Are you in trouble?"

"Just remember what I said, okay?" I gave her a hug and kissed her on the forehead. As I was leaving her room, she stopped me.

"Did Meagan get in yet?" Janaya asked me.

I hesitated again while I was at the door. "No. She's probably just running late." I lied and didn't feel bad in the slightest. I went back to my room and turned my light off before laying across my bed. I stared up at the ceiling still thinking about what I had done. It was eating away at me. Not the fact that I had killed Meagan because in my eyes, that bitch had to go, but the fact that I had taken a life, period. I began to wonder how many lives, if any at all, had my father taken while he was in the streets. Something told me that he had a lot of blood on his hands.

I drifted off and was awakened by loud knocks on the front door and Janaya yelling my name.

"Dah-Dah! It's cops out front and they're knocking on the door!!" She yelled to me from her room. I jumped from my bed and hurriedly threw my slippers on.

"Here I come!" I yelled out as my heart thudded in my chest. I knew what it was about but pretended to be none the wiser. I rubbed my sleepy eyes after I opened the front door and looked the two officers over. "What is it? Is it about my father's murder?" I asked as I looked from one to the other.

The two officers looked at each other and then one took his hat off as he looked at me sympathetically.

"It's not, actually. I'm afraid we have some bad news," the cop said solemnly.

Yani

Janaya came down behind me. "What's going on?"

"There was a robbery earlier at your mother's hair salon. She was found in her office…she'd been shot."

"What…? Is she… is she okay?" Janaya asked sounding as though she was close to tears. She could tell by the look on their faces that the news was not good. She collapsed into me as she burst into tears, screaming why was this happening to us? I put my arms around her as fake tears fell from my eyes.

"When was the last time you heard from her?" one of the cops asked.

"She messaged me to let me know that she couldn't pick me up from the airport, but ordered an Uber for me so I could get home. That was around five something." I told the officer.

"Are you sure it's her? I mean, maybe we should look and see just to be sure," Janaya bellowed through her tears. I held her tighter as I looked at the officer with sympathetic eyes. I could see he was reluctant at first but then nodded his head yes.

I told them that we would be right back before closing the door. Janaya was sobbing uncontrollably until we got to the stairs. She stopped and then turned to me with the coldest look on her face.

"Is this why you said what you said to me earlier?" she asked me. I had never seen her look so angry before. I didn't know what to say to her so I looked at the floor and remained quiet. She punched me in my chest and pushed me.

"How could you do this, Davion?" she hissed in a hushed tone. "We ain't got nobody, now! Who's going to take care of us now, huh? Who?" she wailed on me with her tiny fists.

I grabbed my sister and shook her to calm her down before pinning her to the wall.

"That bitch had to go! She fuckin' set Pops up to be killed with Buck and was fucking that nigga in the kitchen the day of his fucking funeral!"

"I don't believe you!" Janaya cried.

"Yes, yes!" I snarled in her face. We glared at each other and after searching my eyes, I felt Janaya go limp in my arms once she realized I was telling the truth. She looked like her world had come tumbling down as her eyes became teary.

"You need to pull it together before we go identify Meagan's body. We all we got, Jah. This is it. It's just you and me now, no bullshit. You and me. You've gotta have my back on this shit. I need you to. Please…" I pleaded with her.

Janaya nodded her head. I helped her to stand up and we both went upstairs to throw some sweats on and our sneakers before leaving out with the cops to identify Meagan's body.

We rode in silence over to the morgue and followed behind the officer over to where they had Meagan. I put my arm around Janaya as we waited behind a huge glass window. It seemed like an eternity before the coroner finally arrived and Janaya was visibly shaken up.

The coroner looked at us sympathetically before pulling back the sheet. I turned away and closed my eyes as Janaya hollered out. She faced the wall, hitting it with her fist as she cried out in anguish. I wasn't sure if she was that damn good of an actress or if she really was truly upset and in turmoil.

Hoop Dreams Deflated

The officer was speaking to us but I couldn't hear a word he was saying. Flashbacks of the gun going off and Meagan being slumped over her desk partially tormented me.

"We're going to do everything that we can to get to the bottom of this unfortunate incident. Is there someone we can call for you? An aunt or an uncle?" the officer asked us.

"We don't have anybody left!" Janaya cried out in between choking on her sobs. "Our mom is dead! They just killed our dad a few months ago! We don't have anybody… nobody!"

"Unfortunately, since the two of you are minors, I can't release you unless it's into the care of an adult. And if we aren't able to locate a family member or a close family friend who can at least take you for the night and maybe a few days until this is sorted out, we would have to put you both in a group home," the officer informed us.

I hugged Janaya to comfort her and looked at the officer. "There's a woman that looked after us when my mom was going through stuff before she died. Ms. Aretha. Can I call her?"

"Absolutely," the officer nodded.

Yani

I reached in my back pocket and pulled my cell-phone to call Ms. Aretha. She answered sounding groggy and sleepy.

"Hello? Ms. Aretha?" I spoke into the phone.

"Yes… who is this…?"

"Ms. Aretha, it's Davion," I answered as I became choked up.

"Davion, sweetheart, what's wrong? Is everything okay?"

I had to take a few deep breaths before I could get the words out. "Meagan's dead. Someone killed her at the shop."

"Oh, sweet Jesus, Lord cover this family! Haven't these babies been through enough?" I heard Ms. Aretha cry out. I handed the phone to the officer and he spoke with her, briefly explaining what they knew so far and letting her know where we were.

The officer handed me the phone and we were taken to a room where we waited for Ms. Aretha's arrival. A part of me was eaten up with guilt as it never occurred to me that once Meagan was gone, we could possibly be separated and sent into group homes. I began to worry that maybe I acted too hastily and should have thought things out.

Hoop Dreams Deflated

Ms. Aretha was shown into the room we were in and wrapped her arms around the both of us. I could hear her mumbling a prayer through her tears as she held us tightly.

"May I ask what the nature of your relationship to these two is?" another officer asked after giving us a moment.

"I guess I'm their guardian now," Ms. Aretha said in return. "A few days before their father went missing, he stopped by my house and gave me paper work. But I never imagined I would actually need them, especially so soon." She shook her head as she looked at the two of us. "These babies have been through… so much…" she burst into tears as she put her hands to her face. I placed a hand sympathetically on her shoulder not knowing what to say. I wondered if Pops knew… or if he suspected that he and Meagan were targets.

After giving us various numbers to grief counselors and different therapists, we were finally able to leave.

We rode back to Ms. Aretha's house in silence with Janaya resting her head on my shoulder. I grabbed her hand and squeezed it just as I had done while at Pops' and Joselyn's funerals. She squeezed my hand back.

"Would you two like to go home and get a few things so you'll be comfortable?" Ms. Aretha asked when we pulled up in front of her door.

I shook my head no as I rubbed the top of my nose between my eyes to fight off a headache that was brewing. "I just want to go to bed. I can't go back in that house knowing that Pops and Meagan are gone. I can't do it."

"Me neither," Janaya replied softly.

"I understand," Ms. Aretha said to us sympathetically. "Well Janaya, you can take the middle bedroom for now, and Davion, you can sleep in the room with Lamar."

"If it's okay with you Ms. Aretha, can I just sleep on the couch tonight? I kinda just want to be alone." I asked.

"I understand. I need to talk to you in the morning, Davion. But for now, I want you both to know that you will always have a place with me. I've always looked at you two as my children ever since you first started coming by when you were little. If you decide that you would rather stay at your home than here, we'll work something out. You two get some sleep… at least try to."

Janaya nodded her head. Ms. Aretha went upstairs to get us fresh sheets, blankets and pillows. Janaya waited until she was out of ear shot before she turned her eyes to me.

"What did you do?" she asked me.

I shook my head. "Not now, Janaya."

"You need to tell me something!" she hissed.

"You need to lower your voice," I sneered in a low tone. "I said not now. Not in here. It's too much shit that honestly, I think you would be better off if you didn't know. Go to bed." I said firmly.

Janaya stared at me and I could see the disappointment in her eyes. She shook her head and met Ms. Aretha at the top of the stairs to retrieve her blankets before heading to bed. Ms. Aretha then came back downstairs.

"Davion… you're 17 years old now and I know that you've seen way more than your sister has, though you both have had your share of grief. I was going to wait until tomorrow to talk to you, but I think it would be best if I told you now.

Yani

"Your father had several life insurance policies. Joselyn didn't have a life insurance policy when she died and he said he didn't want to make that mistake again. He took out policies for you and your sister and lastly, he had two policies for himself and one for Meagan. For those three, you two are the beneficiaries, but he left me as the trustee." She sighed. "He left you two quite a bit of money… over a million dollars in life insurance money between him and Meagan."

I felt light headed when I heard Ms. Aretha say the amount. Pops knew. Ever since Joselyn's death and I found out that he was a drug dealer, I always blamed him and believed that he chose to live a reckless lifestyle knowing that there were no guarantees. But he knew and understood that. I remembered one of the last things he said to me was that no matter what, me and Janaya would be taken care of so we would never see days like what we went through when we were little living with Joselyn.

I put my hands to my face and began to weep. Not for joy or for relief, but because no amount of money would be enough. I would give up every penny and take living back at the house on Medary street with the roaches and the dark just to have him and Joselyn back. It wasn't enough and never would be.

Ms. Aretha rubbed my back as she told me it would be okay. But I had heard that shit all of my life and it wasn't. Tonight, it felt like it would never be okay.

After I'd calmed down, Ms. Aretha laid me down and pulled a blanket over me. It was the first time I had been tucked in since I was thirteen-years-old after Joselyn died. She gave me two Motrin to help with the migraine that had come on. I nodded off shortly after that.

Though I was asleep, I didn't feel like I was dreaming. It was more like I was reliving the shooting at the salon. I could feel the kick back from the gun and feel the warmth from Meagan's blood as it splattered on my face. But this time, her blood flowed towards me and began to cover me like a second skin suit. I stared at my arms in horror as the blood covered them and moved up my chest, neck and chin towards my mouth. I could taste the salt from her blood and began to scream.

Yani

I jumped from my sleep clutching the blankets, breathing heavily and drenched in sweat. I swung my legs over the edge of the sofa and leaned on my knees as I struggled to catch my breath. Though I didn't feel guilty for killing Meagan, something inside of me felt tormented.

I got up from the sofa and sluggishly made my way up the stairs. I was almost at the top when Lamar's bedroom door opened. Janaya was leaving out in only her t-shirt. Lamar was shirtless. Janaya stood on her tippy toes to kiss him and it didn't look like that was the first kiss between them. She then crept to the room she was supposed to be in and closed the door quietly. Lamar closed his door as well.

Did this nigga just run up in my sister? She had just turned 14 a few weeks before and Lamar wouldn't be 17 until the summer, but still! Every fucking nigga knew my baby sister was off fucking limits. And he of all fucking people knew better. I was so pissed behind what I saw that I forgot about my need to splash cool water on my face and neck. I went back down to the couch to lay back down. I was definitely nipping this shit in the bud in the morning.

I had rolled over on my side and heard my phone vibrate. I thought it might be Tashai checking to make sure I was okay. Instead, it was Sam.

"Young bol, we need to rap tomorrow. Hit me up ASAP,"

I looked at the text and a twinge of fear washed over me. I wondered if he knew about Meagan and suspected me. It's no way. The police were reporting it as a robbery. I had to chill…

Later that morning I awakened to the smell of grits, fish, eggs and toast. Ms. Aretha was whipping up a feast at quarter to six in the morning. She saw when I sat up.

"Good morning, Davion. I'm making breakfast so wash your hands and face and come on and fix you a plate."

I didn't intend to eat but my stomach over ruled that initial idea.

I went upstairs to do as Ms. Aretha said and quickly forgot about the food when I heard music coming from Lamar's room. I peeked in and saw him standing in front of the mirror dressed in his uniform, brushing the waves in his head. I walked into his room and grabbed him, turning him around before slamming him into the wall while gripping him by his collar. He looked startled.

"Yo bruh, what the fuck?!" he said, frightened.

"You know what, nigga! I know you ain't running up in my little sister right up under my fucking nose, yo!" I snarled angrily with spit flying out of my mouth.

"It's not like that…" Lamar tried to explain. But I wasn't trying to hear that shit. I was two seconds away from punching him through the fucking wall when Janaya grabbed my shirt.

"Davion, stop!" she screamed at me.

"What the fuck were you doing coming out of his room last night?" I snapped with my back to her. The room became quiet except for the music coming from Lamar's phone. I let him go with a jerk, pushing him into the wall before turning to Janaya. She opened her mouth to respond but the look on my face shut her up.

"It's not what you think, Davion. Real shit." Lamar tried to explain again.

"Shut the fuck up," I shot back at him as I stared at Janaya coldly. "How long?" I asked her.

She glanced at Lamar and then looked back at me. She then lowered her eyes. "A month."

"A month…a fucking month, Jah-Jah? You been fucking this nigga for a month. You been lying to me for a fucking month!"

"Davion listen, it's not like that. She ain't just some jawn, yo. I'm really feeling her…"

I grimaced at his words and shot him a look so cold he jumped back.

"You weren't around anymore, Davion. Pops was dead and either you were doing your extra classes, at practice, or with Tashai. You weren't there. Lamar was… I didn't lie to you. I just didn't tell you because I didn't want y'all to fight. Y'all are like brothers and I like him. I can't help how I feel! And you can't go around kicking every nigga's ass who likes me, too!"

"Ain't none of these niggas about to have you out here on some hoe-shit. Period! Tell me y'all been using condoms at least?" The silence from both of them almost had me swinging. I turned to Lamar but it was nowhere for him to back up because his ass was already up against the wall.

Yani

"What the fuck, nigga? You trying to get her knocked!" I seethed as I grabbed him by the throat.

"No…" he squealed. Before I knew it, I'd thrown him onto his bed. When I turned to Janaya, she backed away from me. I had never seen her look at me with fear in her eyes before. That look in her eyes stopped me dead in my tracks. I looked her over and shook my head in disgust.

"You said you wasn't like these little fast-ass chicks in these streets. But now you out here fucking around, acting like a hoe just like 'em though." Her mouth hung open, surprised by my words. I ignored her teary eyes as I walked past her, bumping her.

I didn't want anything to eat at that moment. I clamored down the stairs and grabbed my coat.

"Davion, what is the problem?" Ms. Aretha asked me when she saw me heading to the front door.

"Nothing," I answered sharply.

"You're not eating?" she asked me.

"No, I'm not hungry."

"Wait a minute…" she said as she hurried over to me. "It just after 6AM, where are you going?"

I kept my back to her so she couldn't see the hurt in my face. "I need to get some school uniforms so I can go to school. I already missed a week when Pops died. I can't miss too many days or I won't get to graduate early. And with everything going on, I need to get the…" I caught myself before I cursed. I had to blow out air to try to calm down. "I need to get out of here."

"We still need to finish talking about what we were talking about last night."

"Soon as I get out of school, Ms. Aretha. I promise." When she didn't say anything in return, I took that as though she was letting it go and I left her house.

I didn't feel like catching the bus, so I ordered another Uber and had him take me back to my house. As soon as I got inside, I could feel all the pain from losing Pops and killing Meagan. It all came crashing down on me like a ton of bricks. I fell to my knees, crying like a baby.

"That's the thing about guilt. Shit is a muthafucka and creeps up on you when you least expect it." I heard a voice say, making me jump. I

Yani scrambled to my feet, shocked to see Sam standing behind me.

"How…?" I started to ask.

"You didn't lock the door behind yourself when you came in, lil nigga." Sam looked around and then locked the door behind himself. "I told you I would handle things," Sam said as he looked down at me.

"What are you talking about?" I asked as I looked at him confused.

"Come on, Davion. I knew you since you were a little boy. Ya Pops always said your anger was going to get you in some shit he wouldn't be able to get you out of."

"What the fuck are you talking about?" I asked again with base, playing stupid.

"I'm fucking talking about Meagan turning the fuck up dead just hours after I told you what the fuck was going on between her and Buck. The shit is way too obvious. But my question is, where did you put the gun afterwards?"

"You think I did this shit? Are you fucking crazy!? Where the fuck would I get a gun from, huh? What the fuck would I get out of it? Meagan was all we had! She might've been a snake-bitch, but that snake-bitch is what kept me and Janaya together. Now we facing going into a home. We're fucked! We ain't got shit, now! No-fucking-body!" I yelled. "If you know me so well, you should know I would never fuck us like this. You know what my sister means to me." I shook my head at him before plopping down on the couch. I hoped like hell he believed me. "For all we know, Constantine took her ass out to tie up any loose ends with what went down with Pops."

Sam stared at me for a moment as though he was considering what I said. He then took a seat in the chair not too far from me. "How do you know about Constantine?" he asked me.

"Before Pops was killed, him and Meagan were arguing. She mentioned his name and said that she was getting threats at the shop."

Sam looked at me with a raised eye brow. "She said that? Are you sure?"

"Yeah… why?"

Sam stared at me for a moment and then leaned back in his chair. The silence was a bit too much and I wasn't in the mood for any suspenseful shit. "I'ma see what I can dig up. If Meagan was getting threats at the shop, it's possible that her part ain't what it seemed on the surface."

I opened my mouth to mention that was what she said before I shot her, but closed it. "I'ma need you to elaborate."

Sam stood up and headed to the front door. "Meaning, she could have probably figured if she couldn't save your father, she would try to save herself... and you and your sister."

My heart sank into my stomach. The idea that I had killed Meagan wrongly began to eat away at my conscience. I needed justification to kill this guilt. "That doesn't explain her fucking Buck, though."

"Do you play chess?" Sam asked me.

"No. But what does that have to do with anything?" I asked in return.

"In the game of chess, the Queen protects the King and makes any necessary sacrifices to do so... even if that means sacrificing herself." And with those words, Sam left out the house and closed the door behind himself.

I thought on what Sam said as well as what Meagan said before I shot her. *It's not as cut and dry as you think, Davion…"* What the fuck did she mean by that? Now I'll probably never know.

Meagan's funeral was a blur. A lot of people came out to pay their respects. But I noticed that Buck didn't seem too broken up considering the two of them had been fucking for months and she was probably carrying his child. He didn't come to the burial or to the repast. I wondered what was up with that.

Luckily for my sake, the police had no leads in Meagan's murder. The only people who knew what happened was Janaya and me and I never told her exactly what happened. She just knows I did it. Our relationship wasn't the same once I found out about her and Lamar. She barely talked to me. I needed to make it right before I left for USC. Graduation was in two months.

I was sitting at the house with Tashai on my bed with my hands folded together in serious thought. It was easier for us to be together there instead of her house since her mother still wasn't too fond of me. She tugged on my ear before kissing my cheek.

Yani

"You're quiet," she said to me before resting her head on my shoulder.

I shook my head. "Just thinking," I replied in a low tone.

"About what?" she pressed.

"A lot of shit happened this school year. Pops and Meagan were both killed, my best friend is smashing my little sister and our friendship ain't been the same since I found out. Jah-Jah barely talks to me…"

Tashai interrupted me, "You need to apologize to her. You called her a hoe, Davion. That hurt her. You know your sister is far from that."

"I didn't call her a hoe, I said she was acting like one," I argued.

"That's splitting hairs and you know it," she shot back at me. We both fell silent as I thought on what she said. "With everything that's happened to the two of y'all, you should know that life is too short to keep a beef with somebody you love. Talk to her. Because as close as y'all are, it would suck if something else happened before y'all patched things up," Tashai said to me as she traced her finger across my cheek.

I thought about what she said and knew that she was right. "I'll talk to her tonight. I promise." I said to her before giving her a brief kiss.

"What's really bothering you? You haven't been the same since you came back from USC and Meagan was killed."

I looked away from her not wanting Tashai to see the guilt in my eyes. There was no way I could tell her that I had murdered my step-mother. "You sure you can handle me being all the way in California next year?" I asked her instead.

"I'ma miss you a lot but I know this is a good thing. We can FaceTime each other and I'll see you during the holidays. I'm willing to try if you are," she told me.

I nodded my head and looked away. "I never told you what I found in the Vivint footage that I looked up."

"I figured you didn't want to talk about it."

"Mostly, yeah. But it was mainly because of what I found." I fell silent for a minute as I tried to think of what to tell Tashai and how much I shouldn't tell her. "I think Meagan had something to do with my father being killed."

Yani

Tashai looked at me wide eyed and then shook her head in disbelief. "No way. Are you serious? Are you sure?"

"I saw video of her having sex with Pops' best friend who claims he was his right hand man. And she was talking to him saying how now that my father was gone, she wanted more since it was her ass that was on the line or something like that."

"Why didn't you tell the cops, Davion? I mean, you knew all of this for months! Long before Meagan was killed." Tashai said to me in shock.

"Because I ain't no fucking snitch. And I was having a hard time believing this shit my damn self."

"It's not about you being a snitch. It's about making sure that the people who were responsible for your father's murder is caught and your father gets justice." Tashai argued.

"This is bigger than my father's murder. Meagan was a pawn. If I start running my mouth about what I think I know, who's to say that whoever was really behind the shit doesn't come after me thinking I know more than what I really do? I ain't getting killed over some speculation shit."

Tashai fell silent this time as though she was thinking about what I said. I was trying to find a way to get Tashai to help me with something without telling her too much.

"I need you to do something for me," I asked her. I looked her in her eyes so she could see how serious I was.

"Okay…" she replied with hesitation.

"I didn't get a chance to look through the footage from the day our house got tossed or the other footage between Meagan and Buck. If I give you the password, could you be my second set of eyes?"

Tashai sighed in relief. "Thank God. I thought you were going to ask me to do something crazy like hide a murder weapon or something." She chuckled nervously. "Yeah. I can do that for you." She looked at her watch and then got up. "My mom will be home soon, so I gotta go."

I stood up to help her get dressed and then threw on a pair of ball shorts and a t-shirt so I could walk her to the bus stop. I never let her catch the bus home by herself whenever she came to visit me. Pops always taught me to look after the women I cared about, so I saw to it that she made it home safely no matter what. When she got to her door step, I stopped her before she kissed me goodbye.

"You said earlier that life is too short to leave things unsaid," I reminded her.

"Yeah?" she nodded.

"You need to tell your mom what your uncle did to you." I said as I looked at her seriously. I could almost see the wall go up around her. She backed away from me.

"No. We already talked about this, Davion. I can't tell her."

"Shorty, listen to me. How do you think your mom would feel if she found out from someone other than you?"

"That wouldn't happen because the only person who knows besides me and my trifling uncle is you. And you said you're not a snitch."

"This is different," I argued.

"How?!" she asked raising her voice.

"Because you can't sweep this under the rug like it never happened. You might tell yourself that you're over it, but you're not."

"I can't…" Tashai said as she shook her head with tears in her eyes. I gave her a hug and rubbed the back of her neck.

"I got you, Shorty. If you need me to be here with you when you do it, I'll be here. But you can't keep this from your mom anymore. The same way you said whoever killed my father needs to be brought to justice, so does your uncle. What if he does this to someone else?"

Tashai sobbed in my arms for a moment. It took her a few minutes to calm down but she finally gave in. "I'll tell her," she finally said.

"Tonight," I said firmly as I wiped her face. "I'ma talk to my sister tonight. You talk to your mom and then we'll talk afterwards, okay?"

Tashai nodded her head in agreement. I gave her a hug and kiss and waited for her to go in the house before I left to go to Ms. Aretha's house.

When I came inside of the house, Janaya and Lamar were sitting closely on the couch watching Transformers: Dark of the Moon. Lamar looked at me and jumped away from her. Janaya looked at me and I could see the hurt expression on her face. It took a lot for me to swallow my pride and try to accept the fact that my baby sister was no longer a virgin and had a relationship with my best friend.

I walked over to Lamar and stuck my hand out. "What's up, bro?" I spoke.

Lamar looked at me hesitantly before slapping my hand with our trademark handshake. "What's up?" he spoke.

"Ain't shit. Jah-Jah, let me holla at you for a second."

Janaya looked at me startled since that was the most I'd said to her since the confrontation we had in Lamar's bedroom over a month before. She got up and we headed up to the room she slept in. I closed the door behind me and we stood in the room, neither of us knowing what to say.

"I'm sorry I called you a hoe…" I finally said.

"You was dead wrong for that Dah-Dah!" Janaya said with tears in her eyes. "Lamar is the only boy I've been with. I ain't never been about that hoe life. All the girls you've had, you should look in the mirror if you wanna know what a hoe looks like!"

"Ouch…" I winced. "I deserved that. I know you're not a hoe. You're my little sister. I just wanted you to hold onto your virginity as long as possible. You ain't mature enough." Janaya shook her head and crossed her arms over her chest. "I can't stop what you already started. Just use condoms, man. Pops would roll over in his grave if you popped up pregnant at 14 and had to put off college and your goals because you were being careless."

Janaya nodded her head. She then gave me a big hug almost knocking me back. "I missed my Dah-Dah," she said as she buried her face in my chest. "Sorry I called you a fake-ass LeBron," she said with a giggle.

"Damn, that's how you feel!" I said before laughing.

"You shouldn't have called me a hoe."

"You right," I agreed. We went back downstairs and I could see Janaya blushing when she sat next to Lamar. When I thought about it, Janaya was safer with him than she was with any of these other knuckle heads that had been trying their luck with her.

"Alright nigga, you had enough time to practice. Come on so I can bust your ass in some 2-K."

Yani

Lamar burst out laughing as he got up from the sofa. He playfully pulled Janaya's ponytail as he walked past her and we ran upstairs to his room to play the game. Things were getting back to normal. I had my baby sister back, I had my home boy back, and in a few months, I would be graduating and heading to USC to start my dream career.

4ᵗʰ Quarter

It was a few days before my graduation and a week before Janaya's graduation. I had gotten the final letter from USC finalizing my acceptance. I sat on the edge of my bed holding the letter, reading it again and again. I wanted nothing more than to have my father next to me, telling me how proud he was of me at that moment. Tear drops fell onto the paper as I held it and I quickly wiped them away. I heard a knock at the door and used my shirt to wipe my eyes.

"Yo!" I answered. My door opened and Janaya peeped her head in.

"Are you busy?" she asked me.

I looked at my watch and saw that it was time for me to go up to the school to get my cap and gown. "Actually, I gotta grab my cap and gown real quick. Can this wait until I get back?"

Yani

Janaya looked disappointed but nodded her head. I threw my arm around her shoulder and we walked down the steps together.

"One more week and you'll officially be a high school student. Time to play with the big boys," I joked.

"Yeah," she replied. She didn't sound as cheerful as I thought she would.

"What's good, Jah-Jah? I thought you would've been hype to walk down the aisle."

"It's nothing…" Janaya said hesitantly. "I just wish Pops could see me walk."

"I know, Jah. I was just thinking about that upstairs in my room while I was looking at my letter. We gon' talk when I get home."

"Okay," she nodded before laying on the couch. I left out the house and made my way over to the 6 bus stop so I could get to Central. Lamar said he'd meet me there after he got off of work and we would hang out for a bit.

I was about to put my earphones in my ear and call Tashai but got a funny feeling. Instead, I tucked my phone in my back pocket. She ended up not having to tell her mother about what her uncle had done to her. Her mother heard our conversation on the steps through their Vivint system. Just like Tashai suspected, it almost destroyed her mother to know that her only daughter was being molested by her uncle at the same time her husband was being murdered. It took a lot of convincing from me and her mother to get her to testify against her uncle. Sadly, she wasn't the only one. He'd also molested two of her cousins. But with her having the courage to speak up, that gave them the courage to speak out against what was done to them as well.

Between going to a therapist to help her get through that tragedy and being prepped for her case against her uncle, she wasn't able to start looking at the footage until a couple of days before.

I was about to cross at Ogontz avenue and Medary street when a car coming towards me began to slow down.

"Psst, Dah-Dah!" I heard a not so friendly voice say. I looked in the direction the voice was coming from and saw a guy pull a gun.

"Oh shit!" I yelled before I took off running. Gun shots rang out and I ducked before I zig

Yani

zagged in between cars. I then ran right in the middle of Ogontz avenue, hoping they wouldn't be bold enough to continue shooting as cars were coming. But they were. Just as a UPS truck was coming, I quickly ran behind it and dove under a car. Glass cut my arm and I bust my lips. I breathed heavily as I hid under the car. Things quieted down but I stayed under the car to make sure the coast was clear.

Somebody had just shot at me. But for the fuck what?! Could it be that someone suspected I was the one who killed Meagan and was retaliating? It couldn't be. Even the cops were stumped and I'd gotten rid of the gun and the clothes I wore that night.

I got from under the car after I was sure all was good and hurried back to the house. The front of my shirt was filthy, as were my sneakers and my arm and knees were bleeding from when I dove under the car. People looked at me strangely and whispered, but I didn't give a shit. It was obvious that I was scared out of my mind by the way I kept checking behind myself and looking around. As soon as I got to the corner of Ms. Aretha's block, I hauled-ass to her house. When I got inside, I quickly closed the door and locked it. I looked out the window, peeking from behind the curtain, still scared shitless and breathing heavily.

Janaya sat up and looked at me. "I thought you were getting your cap and gown," she said to me.

"You ain't just hear them gunshots?" I asked her as I continued to peep from behind the curtains.

"What gunshots?!" Janaya shrieked as she sat up.

I ignored her question as I continued to look out of the window. I wasn't sure if it was my paranoia or if this burgundy Altima had really driven by the house three times. I finally got out of the window and turned to go upstairs. Janaya gasped when she saw me.

"Davion, what happened to you?!"

"I told you, they were shooting. I ran and hid under a car," I told her. I didn't want to tell her that they were shooting at me.

She looked at me suspiciously and I felt like that's what she was thinking. She snatched up the

Yani

paper towels and rushed over to me. "Your arm is bleeding," she said to me.

I winced when she touched me. Until that moment, I didn't feel any pain, but suddenly my knees and arm felt like they were on fire.

"I'm alright," I told her as I moved away from her. "I'ma go take a shower. I'll get my cap and gown in the morning." Janaya stared at me as I went upstairs. I could tell she was worried, but I would rather not say anything than to lie to her and tell her everything would be okay. Those words seemed to be the kiss of death... literally.

As I took a hot shower, I had begun to wish that I hadn't gotten rid of the gun that I used to kill Meagan. Shit, I'd rather be judged by twelve than carried by six.

I got out of the shower and went in Lamar's room so I could get dressed. I was still shaken up but had calmed down a little. As I looked at myself in the mirror, I checked my arm and saw where close to my shoulder had a six-inch cut on it. My knees were skinned but didn't look nearly as bad as my arm. I grabbed my phone and called Tashai.

"Hey, I was just about to call you. What's up?" she spoke cheerfully into the phone.

"I've been thinking about what you said a couple months ago, about me snitching to the cops about Meagan. How soon do you think you'll be able to look at the footage to see who was in the house the day it was ransacked?" I asked hastily.

Tashai fell silent. "Are you sure you want to do that, Davion? Because that would mean the cops would want to look at the footage from y'all Vivint system. And if they look at it, they'll see that you really weren't home all night the night Meagan was killed…"

My heart raced as her words hung in the air. Shit, could she know? I wasn't sure if I should say anything in response so I waited for her to say something else.

"Davion?" she spoke. "Why'd you lie about being home that night?"

I sighed deeply. "Tashai, I can't…"

"Shush… don't say anything because I don't want to know. Even though I'm pretty sure why you lied, it would be better for me if you just

Yani

didn't say anything. Why do you need the footage so fast now?"

"Someone just shot at me," I whispered into the phone.

"What!" Tashai shrieked.

This time, I shushed her. "I don't know who it was."

"You didn't get a look at him?" she asked quickly.

"All I saw was a big fucking gun, that's it. When I saw it, I ran and zig-zagged in between some cars and then hid under one." I explained.

"Where are you now?" Tashai asked.

"I'm at Ms. Aretha's house." I told her as I peeked out of Lamar's window.

"Okay. I'm on my way home. I'll look through the footage and try to get something as fast as I can. You really need to go to the cops."

"I will. I'ma send you a picture of that nigga Buck. If he's in the house the day it got tossed, send a screen shot to me and then I'll go to the cops."

"Okay, I will. Just be careful. Please. Stay in the house."

"I will. I promise." I disconnected the call and sat on the edge of the bed with my hands to my head. A part of me felt like I was running out of time. But I was determined to make it to USC... by any means necessary.

I closed my eyes thinking back to right before the bullets started flying. *"Dah-Dah..."* I remembered the voice calling to me. Not too many people call me by that name. This was someone that knew me and knew me well. It didn't sound like Buck's pussy ass. I wished like shit I had gotten a look at who it was.

The next morning, Ms. Aretha took me to pick up my cap and gown. My prom pictures as well as my year book were there also. I stared at the picture of me and Tashai. I couldn't take my eyes off it, namely her. She looked beautiful. If I were a puzzle, she was my missing pieces. We fit perfectly.

"You two look amazing together." Ms. Aretha said, snapping me out of my thoughts. "She's a very beautiful and smart young lady."

"Yeah..." I said in return. I pulled the mirror down and put my cap on to see how I looked. As

Yani

I stared at myself, I could see where I looked just like Pops; a younger, slimmer version, but I looked just like him. For some reason, it was hard for me to look at myself. I slid my cap off and pushed the mirror back into its place.

"Can we stop at my father's house for a minute?" I asked.

"Sure," Ms. Aretha replied. We drove to the house in silence. It had been more than a month since I had been there. The living room furniture was all covered with white sheets. The floors were dull from not being buffed like Pops had them done regularly every month. I walked through looking around. The place that once was my home felt like an empty shell. And even though the house was mine now, automatically paid off upon Pops' death, I didn't want it.

I looked on the wall at our family photo and the other family photos on the mantel. Seeing Pops in those photos and knowing that he wouldn't get to see his oldest and only son walk down the aisle tomorrow as well as his daughter transition to high school brought out a rage in me. I snatched the big family portrait off the wall and grabbed one of the fireplace pokers and began using it to knock the photos and nick-nacks from the mantel. I wasn't satisfied so I went over to the China cabinet and kicked the glass in before using the poker to smash the other glass. Flashes of sitting in Joselyn's living room with Janaya and hearing her tell me she was hungry went through my mind causing me to tear more shit up in a rage. I saw Janaya getting pushed when we were jumped coming from the store, and then the confrontation I had with Joselyn before finding her on the couch with the needle in her arm. All of those flashes went through my mind sending me into a blind rage. I trashed the downstairs, smashing and breaking up whatever I could. I didn't stop until the memory of Pops telling me I was a better man than he could have ever hoped to be came to me. Remembering him telling me that the night before he went missing caused me to break down in tears.

"The only reason I didn't stop you is because I know that there are no words to comfort you or console you, Davion. You've seen more and witnessed more tragedy than people twice your age." I heard Ms. Aretha say from behind me. "I

Yani

can't tell you it will get any easier… you just gotta take it one day at a time, baby. One day at a time," she said sympathetically.

I dropped the poker and leaned onto the back of one of the dining room chairs. My heart ached and my body shook as I tried to calm down. After I was able to get myself under control, I walked past Ms. Aretha and went back to the car without saying anything. We rode back to the house in silence. I flipped through my yearbook for the most part of the day until Janaya came home from school. She had gotten her yearbook as well.

"How come you ain't get anybody to sign it?" she asked me as she looked in it.

"I didn't even think about it. I'll get people to sign it at the graduation party. You know everybody and their mom gon' be at this jawn," I smirked. I flipped through a few more pages and then sat her book to the side. "What was it that you wanted to talk to me about yesterday?" I asked her.

Janaya suddenly looked nervous and began fidgeting. When she opened her mouth to speak, my phone went off with a call from Tashai.

"Hold up one second," I said to Janaya, putting my finger up. "Hey, babe…"

"I'll come back later," Janaya said before getting up quickly and rushing out of Lamar's room.

"You okay?" Tashai asked.

"Why'd you ask?" I replied as I leaned back on Lamar's bed.

"I… I saw the footage of you at the house earlier. If you need me, I can come over," she offered.

I wanted to see her badly. But I didn't want to take the chance of something happening to her while she was down here.

"No," I told her. "I'll see you tomorrow after my graduation. Your mom still letting you come, right?"

"Yeah, I'll be there. I gotta run home right afterwards because my mom has a delivery coming and she doesn't want it to get sent back. But I'm still coming to your party.'

"Okay, cool." I said in return as I closed my eyes. It was silent on the phone for a moment which was fine with me. I would have rather been

Yani

laying on Tashai's chest listening to her breathe though.

"You're not sleep are you?" Tashai asked me.

"Nah, I'm not sleep, babe. I'm still here." I told her. "I got the prom pics back today."

"Yeah?" Tashai replied excitedly. "Take a pic of them and send it to me. I hope I don't look crazy."

"Nah, you look beautiful, babe. I'ma send you a pic and then get something to eat. Call me later on." I told her as I heard a knock at the door.

"Okay," she said softly. I disconnected the call and stood at the top of the steps listening.

"Davion isn't here," I heard Ms. Aretha say even though she had just brought me home.

"Oh, he's not?" I heard an unfamiliar voice say in response. "I thought I just saw him come in here."

Lamar went over to the door near his mother. "Nah homie, you saw me come in. He ain't here." Lamar said in an intimidating voice I had never heard him use before.

The guy looked from Ms. Aretha to Lamar and nodded his head before leaving. Ms. Aretha closed the door and locked it. I could tell by the look on her face that she was shaken up. I came the rest of the way downstairs and looked at both of them wondering why they told whoever that was at the door that I wasn't here.

"What's going on?" I asked.

Ms. Aretha looked at me and I could tell she was upset. "Carrie told me earlier that the shooting that happened yesterday was some guys shooting at you. You wanna tell me what the hell is going on?"

I was stumped and not sure what to say so I shrugged my shoulders. "I don't know what to tell you."

"You can start by telling me whether or not Carrie was telling the truth. Were they shooting at you yesterday or not?"

I looked at Lamar and then looked at the floor. "Yes." I mumbled.

"For what?!" Ms. Aretha practically screamed.

"What happened?" Lamar asked.

"I was on my way to get my cap and gown and when I went to cross Ogontz, this car pulled up and somebody called my name. When I

Yani

looked, I saw the gun and started running. I'm zig-zagging in between cars and shit and they still bussing at me. So then this UPS truck was coming, so I cut behind it and crawled under a car."

"This shit is crazy!" Lamar exclaimed as he threw his hands in the air.

"Watch your mouth." Ms. Aretha snarled at her son. She then turned to me. "You should have said something so we could call the cops. Do you have any idea why they would be shooting at you?"

I looked at Ms. Aretha for a space of heartbeats. I was terrified that it could come out that I killed Meagan. I didn't want to go to jail. But I didn't want to be killed either.

"Because I might know who killed my father. Or at least who had him killed." I finally admitted.

Lamar and Ms. Aretha looked at me stunned. The room held the kind of silence that was so thick, you could slice through it with a knife. I happened to look behind me and noticed Janaya was on the step.

"How long have you been sitting on this information? Never mind that. Who do you think it is?" Ms. Aretha asked as she leaned into the sofa arm for support, probably so she didn't pass out.

"I overheard Meagan talking to my dad's best friend Buck. She sent my Dad to take care of something and Buck had him snatched from there. I think Buck did it so he could be the distributor for their drug business. Meagan was sleeping with Buck, too."

"This is too much," Ms. Aretha stated as she put her hand to her face. "Okay, so if Meagan and Buck knew what you knew, is it possible that he killed Meagan to keep her quiet and is coming for you next."

I shrugged. There was no way I was going to elaborate on her speculation.

"We need to call the cops," Ms. Aretha said as she grabbed her phone.

"No!" I yelled. "If we call the cops tonight, I'll miss graduation tomorrow. With everything that's happened, I can't miss this. Despite all the shit I went through this year, I still managed to keep my grades up and graduate early so I can make it to USC. I earned this." I said to Ms.

Yani

Aretha. "We'll call after the graduation party when everybody leaves."

"I'll give you that. But right after, we're going to go straight to the police station and you are telling them everything. I don't wanna hear anything about that no snitching code you kids have these days. Your life depends on you telling everything you know!" Ms. Aretha said to me firmly.

I nodded my head in agreement.

"Davion, can we talk real quick?" Janaya asked me.

I turned to Janaya and remembered she had been trying to talk to me for the last few days. I followed her up to her room and she closed the door behind us.

"What's good, Jah-Jah?" I asked as I sat on her bed.

"Do you think it's Uncle Buck that shot at you?" Janaya asked.

"I don't know. And that ain't what you wanted to talk to me about, so what's really up?"

Janaya started playing with her nails and wouldn't look at me. That was a sign that she was in trouble. I stared at her for a moment and looked her over.

"Yo, talk Jah-Jah." I said firmly.

"Promise me you won't get mad at me first." Janaya said. I could hear the desperation in her voice.

"Depends on what you're about to tell me," I said in return.

Janaya stared at me for a minute and then took a deep breath. "I'm pregnant."

Dead silence. The room was so quiet I was positive I could hear that emergency broadcast beeping sound.

"What the fuck did you just say?"

"I'm sorry, Davion. I'm so sorry…" Janaya said in tears.

"Wait… you didn't just say what the fuck I think you just said. Tell me you did NOT just say that shit."

Janaya put her hands to her face and began to let out uncontrollable sobs. I was pissed. I was hot. I can't say that she knew better because she's just a kid. Lamar knew better but I couldn't fully put the blame on him. I was so consumed with trying to figure out the part Meagan played in Pops' murder that I hadn't been looking out for her like I had always promised to do. Like she said, I wasn't there and Lamar was.

I stood up and wrapped my arms around Janaya. She began to cry harder and I honestly didn't know what to say to her. All I could think to do was rub her back and shush her. How could I be there for her when I was going to be all the way over in California while she was pregnant?

"Did you tell Lamar yet?" I asked her.

"No," she mumbled through her sobs.

"Okay, well you need to tell him sooner than later. Matter of fact…" I opened the bedroom door and Janaya grabbed my arm.

"No, what are you doing? Stop Davion." Janaya pleaded.

"Either you tell him now, or I'm telling Ms. Aretha that y'all been fucking in her house for months. Now which one do you want to deal with now?" I said in a low tone. Janaya piped down and plopped down on her bed with her hands to her face as she shook her leg.

"Yo Mar, come here real quick, bruh." I called to Lamar.

Lamar peeped his head out of his room and then came down the hall.

"What's up, homie?" he asked me.

"Come in here real quick." I said to him as I stood to the side so he could come into the room. I closed the door behind us and leaned into it. Lamar looked at both of us confused.

"What's going on?" Lamar asked.

"Go 'head, Jah. Tell 'em." I said as I crossed my arms over my chest. On God, if Lamar came out his mouth on some the baby ain't mine shit or even hinted at an abortion, I was going to beat the brakes off his ass.

I listened as Janaya managed to tell him that she was pregnant. Lamar looked like he'd lost all the color in his face and was going to pass out. I watched as he walked over to my sister and hugged her assuring her that it was going to be alright and that he would man up and take care of his responsibility. My man. He then stood up and came over to me.

"I gotta come to you as a man just like I would if it was her father I had to face," Lamar replied.

Yani

"You better be glad it ain't Pops that you gotta face 'cause he would've knocked your ass smooth the fuck out." I said half-way joking.

"I know, right? Look man, like I told you when you first found out, your sister ain't just some jawn to me. I really care about her and I'ma do right by her. I promise you. That's my word." Lamar assured me. I nodded my head as I shook his hand.

"You better mean that shit 'cause it ain't a problem for me to come all the way the fuck from Cali to bust that ass." We both laughed but he knew I was dead-ass serious.

"We gon' have to hold off on telling my mom, though. She's already hot about that situation with you, Davion. One crisis at a time, feel me?" Lamar said to us both.

"That's cool with me." I said in return.

I went back downstairs and sat back on the couch. Graduation was tomorrow and I couldn't wait. I sent the prom picture to Tashai like I promised and then got something to eat. After showering and laying out my cap and gown with my slacks, dress shirt and shoes, I called Tashai and talked on the phone with her for almost three hours before she started to fall asleep.

"My bad, I'm all falling asleep on you. I'ma let you go so you can get some sleep before your graduation tomorrow," she said to me.

"No don't hang up. I can't lay next to you and listen to you breathe so this is the next best thing," I said to her in a sleepy voice.

"Awww," Tashai gushed before giggling. We said a few more words to each other and then I knew she had fallen asleep by the sound of her breathing. I closed my eyes and listened to her.

"You're my peace in a world filled with tragedy. If I were an incomplete puzzle, you'd be my missing pieces. I love you, babe." I said to her. I waited a moment before disconnecting our call so I could go to sleep. As I was plugging my phone up so it could charge, a text message came through.

"I love you, too." Tashai texted with two heart eyed emoji faces. I sent two back in return and went to sleep.

The next morning, I made sure I showered before everyone. As I was brushing my teeth,

Yani

Janaya barged in the bathroom and threw up in the toilet. I gagged before I spit my toothpaste in the sink and slammed the bathroom door closed.

"Yo, what the fuck? You trying to get caught?" I asked her.

She coughed and gagged as she shook her head. "No. But Ms. Aretha is cooking something with onions and I can't take the smell." Janaya whined.

"Well, you better get that shit under control. Get out so I can finish getting ready. Hope you don't get all car sick on the way to the graduation. Fuck around and puke on my damn clothes." I burst out laughing as Janaya left the bathroom.

"That's not funny," she said as she gave me the evil eye.

After getting dressed and throwing on my cap and gown, Ms. Aretha began snapping a lot of pictures. We took a group selfie and then I had Janaya take one of me by myself so I could send it to Tashai. She texted me back telling me how proud she was of me.

At the graduation, I was honored for graduating early with honors, and heading to USC on a full athletic scholarship. When it was time to walk across the stage to receive my diploma I shook the principal's hand before getting on my knees. I promised I wouldn't cry but not having Pops and Joselyn there hurt my heart. I kissed my two fingers and pointed them to the sky as my way of saluting them. The audience, most of which who knew what I had gone through that year cheered loudly for me and stood to their feet. I heard Janaya scream from the crowd for me to hit the folks and I began milly rocking sending the crowd into an uproar. I left the stage slapping some of the other seniors and teachers high-fives and giving out hugs. Today was definitely a huge day and I hoped that Pops and Joselyn were looking down on me smiling and proud.

At the let out, I had to get through a sea of people who were stopping me to tell me how proud they were of me. There was also a camera man from ABC News with the same journalist who did his brief interview with me in front of the house when Pops was missing. He asked me a few questions for another quick interview except this time, I was much more pleasant.

Yani

Janaya ran over to me and gave me a big hug. "I got next!" she shouted, referring to her graduation that was exactly one week later. She showed me the video she took of me walking across the stage and dancing and I laughed. Ms. Aretha got her paparazzi on and then I finally saw Tashai. I couldn't wait to get to her. I yanked her to me and kissed her longingly. She broke out kiss when she heard people whistling at us and then buried her face in my chest to hide her blushing. Ms. Aretha was kind enough to take her home and then we went back to her house so we could get ready for the party. Practically everybody was going to be there from school, even some of my original classmates from my junior class.

I quickly changed out of my slacks and shoes and threw on my new Jordans with a new Polo shirt and pair of Gap sweatpants. I didn't plan on getting flashy because I knew I was going to be dancing and partying my ass off. Tashai called me as I was putting on some cologne.

"Hey babe," I spoke into the phone as I checked my appearance in the mirror.

"Hey. I'm still waiting for the UPS man to deliver this package. I just wanted to let you know that I'm still coming," she told me.

"You better." I teased. "What'chu doing right now?" I plopped down on Lamar's bed and began looking at the pictures that Janaya sent to me from the graduation and the let out. She got some pretty good ones. If she decided against playing ball over seas, she definitely could be successful at photography. I never would have thought to take pictures the way she did with her iPhone. The way she faded out the background and kept the main people in the picture in focus was dope.

"I was going through the footage on your Vivint account again. Oh yeah, is it okay if my cousin comes to the party? She's on her way over now and wanted to come through."

"Yeah, she can come through. That's cool with me. If she's cute, she better be ready for them niggas to be on her top," I said with a laugh.

"I bet…" Tashai said softly. She then became quiet. "What the heck…?" she said.

"What, what's wrong?" I asked.

Yani

"I almost dropped my laptop and when I went to grab it, I was able to zoom in to get a better look of the people in the house. I didn't know I could do that. Buck is definitely in there, though..."

"I fucking knew it!" I seethed.

"This other guy looks familiar, too… Like I've seen him somewhere before, but I'm not sure where." Tashai said, sounding more like she was thinking out loud. "Hold up, my cousin just rang the doorbell."

I was just about to ask her to tell me where she thought she knew the other guy from when Ms. Aretha called for me to run to the store to get more ice while Lamar lit the grill.

"Yo, call me right back." I said to Tashai before I disconnected the call.

I went downstairs and met Ms. Aretha in the kitchen which was loaded with a bunch of pre-cooked food. I swear, she could have made a killing as a caterer.

"Ay yo Ms. Aretha, you ever think of starting your own catering company or selling dinners. I swear you'd make a killing mad quick." I said to her as I grabbed a wing ding to taste.

"The thought crossed my mind now and again but it never made it past a mere thought," she chuckled. "But now that Lamar is almost out of school and I don't have any more babies besides your sister, I think I might try my hand at it in a year or so."

I cleared my thought after her comment, thinking of Janaya's pregnancy. "What did you need me to get from the store?" I asked instead.

"I need about three more bags of ice. You think you'll be able to carry them back here real quick?"

"I got'chu, Ms. Aretha." I said waving her money off.

"Thanks sweet-boy. Be careful," she said to me as I headed to the door.

"I will, I promise." I jogged back to her and gave her a kiss on the cheek making her giggle. I then left out of the house and began walking around the corner to the store. My phone rang and I saw that it was Tashai.

"Hey babe, what's up? Did UPS get there yet?"

Yani

"Davion, what is the name of the guy that was at your father's funeral? He was standing next to Buck crying super hard.

"Sam, why?"

"I told you his name is Sam," I heard Tashai say to someone.

"Yo, that nigga name is not Sam. Jo-Jo sell for that nigga and I ain't never heard him call that nigga Sam," a female said in the background.

"Wait, who are you talking to Tashai?"

"My cousin says she knows the guy in the video," Tashai told me.

"Put her on the phone," I said to her.

A chick got on the phone. "Hello?"

"Yeah, who 'dis?" I asked.

"I'm Tashai's cousin Marvela. This nigga in the video name is not Sam, yo."

"What he look like?" I asked as I stopped briefly in the middle of the sidewalk.

"He a skinny nigga with a goatee, sleepy eyes and got a scar on his forehead," Marvela described to me.

"Oh, we know that nigga as Sam. What'chall call 'em."

Hoop Dreams Deflated

"His name is Constantine," she said in a matter of face tone.

I heard a buzzing in my ear as I heard what Marvela said echoing again and again. *"His name is Constantine..."* My heart thudded in my chest as I saw a guy coming towards me. The mean mug expression on his face let me know he wasn't hardly a friend. I began to back up when I saw another guy coming from across the street.

"Fuck..." I mumbled. "Tell Tashai I love her..."

"Be careful..." I heard Ms. Aretha say to me.

"I will... I promise..." I lied before leaving the house.

I turned to run, but no matter how fast I moved my legs, I couldn't pick up speed. It felt like I was moving in slow motion.

"Ignore what you can't conquer... Conquer what you can't ignore..." I heard my father's voice.

"Who do you think got me strung out on this shit in the first place... your fucking father..." Joselyn's voice echoed in my ear.

"So the way I see it, he got what the fuck he deserved... karma..." I heard Joselyn's sister say.

Yani

"I'm glad I got my Dah-Dah back…" Janaya voice sounded off in my ears.

Gun fire erupted. I tried to duck between cars like I had done before but was too slow. I felt something hot hit my leg like an explosion and I stumbled. My mind screamed for me to try to keep running but I was moving even slower than before. Another hot explosion in my arm and another in my back.

"I'm burning… I'm burning!" was all I could think as I tried to crawl away from whoever was shooting at me. *"Daddy, HELP ME! Please Dad, don't let them get me!!!"*

My back felt like it was on fire and I could taste the salt from my blood in my mouth. I thought it was over and prayed the ambulance got to me in time.

"Pussy!" I heard an angry male voice say before more gun fire. One-two-three-four-five-six-seven-eight…

I laid still praying that they would believe I was dead and stop. My back felt like it was on fire and blood was getting in my mouth more and more. I could hear screams and see people crowding around me.

"Oh shit, that's Davion yo! Yo, somebody shot Davion! Oh my fucking God, yo! They killed Davion!" I heard somebody scream.

"But I'm not dead, though…" I thought to myself.

"Davion," I heard my father's voice. *"Son, it's okay. You fought hard. It's alright, now."*

"Pops," I murmured. But it didn't sound like my voice. It sounded more like me when I was five. *"Can I stay with you?"* my five-year-old voice squealed. I saw my father reach his hand out to me and I grabbed it. He scooped me up in his arms and I wrapped my tiny arms around his neck and my legs around his back. I looked back at myself and saw as Lamar held Janaya back who was hysterical. I stared at her for a moment and then looked back at myself just as the cops were placing a white sheet over me. I clung to Pops as he carried me away and for the first time in a long time, I felt safe.

Yani

Four Years Later

A young lady sat nervously in her chair.

Her tassel dangled from her cap and gown with the lights shining on it caused the number 19 to glisten and sparkle. She fidgeted with her hands before looking down at a ring on her finger. When her row was signaled, she took a deep breath and stood up in her five inch stilettos. She took another deep breath and ran her fingers through her hair before moving behind the people in front of her. One by one, names were called and she inched closer to the stage.

"Amber Jones… Curtis Jones…. Derrick… Jones… Janaya Jones…"

Janaya lifted the bottom of her cap and gown up as she made her way up the stairs. A burst of loud cheers from her peers erupted in the Hall where her 12th grade graduation was being held.

She walked over to the principal and shook her hand before giving her a big hug.

"Congratulations, sweetie. I am so proud of you!" the principal said in her ear before letting her go.

"Thank you," Janaya replied as she became teary eyed. She kissed her three fingers and pointed them to the sky just as her brother had done four years prior. She then broke out in the same dance that he had done adding her own twist to it before jumping up as she threw her fist in the air.

"Say yaaaay, mommy," Lamar said as he bounced their three-and-a-half-year-old daughter on his lap.

"Yaaay mommy!" Joselyn said in her sweet voice as she clapped her hands.

"Janaya Jones, is number three in her class and is graduating with honors. She will be continuing her education at USC with a four-year athletic scholarship," the principal boasted. She had watched Janaya come through Central high-school and looked after her making sure she

Yani

stayed focused and didn't let her brother's murder cause her to give up on her own life.

After the graduation, Janaya, Lamar, Ms. Aretha and Tashai along with her three-year-old son Davion Jr. met back at Janaya's home in Mount Airy. With Davion being murdered just around the corner from Ms. Aretha's house, Janaya was adamant about not sleeping another night in that house. Ms. Aretha respected her wishes and moved them into the house Pops left Davion, which by default, went to Janaya.

Janaya didn't want a big graduation. She only wanted a few select friends and her family. She hung her Diploma on the wall next to Davion's and stared at them both as her eyes got teary.

"I did it, Dah-Dah. I did it…" she burst into tears and gripped the mantel to keep herself from collapsing but her knees buckled and she crumbled to the floor.

Lamar knelt next to her as he waved his mother to take their daughter on the porch. Janaya laid her head on his shoulder as she wept.

"Four years ago to the day I wore a white dress to my graduation and right afterwards, I had to change into a black dress to bury my only brother," Janaya bellowed. "They took everything from me."

"Not everything, babe. You got me. We got a beautiful little girl, and you have Davion's son. Despite everything, you made it. You're still standing." Lamar said to her before kissing her forehead.

Janaya nodded her head as she began to calm down. She shifted in his arms and kissed him. "I don't think I could've gotten through any of this without you. I love you."

"I love you, too babe." Lamar said in return before lifting her hand with her engagement ring on it and kissing it. He helped her stand up just as Ms. Aretha was coming in the house.

"Janaya, there's a guy at the door for you with flowers," she said to her.

"Thanks, mom." Janaya replied. She wiped her face and then walked to the door with Lamar. Tashai sent her son in the house to play with little Joselyn. He was the splitting image of Davion. She then stood outside with Lamar and Janaya.

"The flowers are beautiful," Janaya beamed as she smelled them. She then cut her eyes at the

Yani

delivery man. "I take it the job is complete," she said in low tone.

"Yes, ma'am," the delivery man replied. "Everything was finalized this morning."

"And you're positive nothing will trace back this way." Lamar checked.

"I left no loose ends. Everything went smooth and neat like you requested. The have a better chance of finding Jimmy Hoffa than finding them two," the delivery man reassured.

Janaya smiled and then looked at Tashai. Tashai reached in her back pocket and gave him a debit card.

"The money was sent as a donation to your non-profit organization, Fathers for the Streets." Tashai said to him. The Delivery Man took the debit card and swiped it on a hand-held device to make sure the funds were there. When he was satisfied he shook each of their hands and left quietly.

"I'm starving," Janaya said before locking arms with Lamar and Tashai. They laughed as they headed into the house. Janaya looked behind herself and up at the sky. "That's a beautiful sunset… Sleep well, Joselyn, Pops and Davion…"

www.ingramcontent.com/pod-product-compliance
Lightning Source LLC
Chambersburg PA
CBHW072202130726
47910CB00011B/1782